THE GIRL WHO STOLE THE APPLE

A gripping suspense thriller full of twists

PETER TICKLER

Published 2016 by Joffe Books, London.

www.joffebooks.com

© Peter Tickler

ISBN- 978-1-911021-77-3

For Fiona, who eats (but doesn't steal) apples.

CHAPTER ONE

The first thing the girl did after entering the shop was to spin a graceful pirouette. She was wearing a full length dress — blue bodice, short blue sleeves slashed with red, a yellow skirt that billowed around her, with a red band tied in a bow over her sculpted black curls. The woman behind the till noticed her and smiled. Who wouldn't smile when Snow White entered their shop? Not that it was her shop really. She was only doing a four-hour shift to eke out her pension, but Mr Patel had gone home at seven p.m. as usual and Miss Rogers had 'popped out' to check on her father, so for a few minutes it was Mrs Gupta's own personal domain.

The girl made a curtsy, not to Mrs Gupta, but to the stack of special offer foods that greeted customers as they walked in. The automatic doors slid shut and then almost immediately open again. A man in a Che Guevara T-shirt, baseball cap and skinny jeans stood there, swaying on his feet.

Mrs Gupta gave a tut of disapproval. Not that the girl's father — if that was who he was — seemed to notice. His eyes were raised slightly upwards, as if something on the top shelf had caught his eye.

'What sort of father brings a little girl out shopping at that time of night?' she told DS Johnson later. 'She should have been tucked up and asleep long ago.'

'Quite,' he said. Johnson's voice was flat and nasal. From the Midlands she thought, though she was hardly an expert. His suit was off-the-peg and rather too shiny. She noticed things like that because hand-made suits had been the family business until her father had died and her husband had gambled away the profits and then done a runner. The suit was dark grey without even the thinnest stripe and Johnson wasn't wearing a tie either. Not a very classy detective. Nothing like that posh one on TV who spoke such lovely Queen's English.

'Do you have children?' Mrs Gupta asked. She was a past master at turning a simple conversation into a rambling Odyssey.

'What happened next?' said the detective, ignoring her question.

Mrs Gupta frowned. What *had* happened next? It wasn't as if it had been that long ago. She had been kept in hospital overnight, 'just for observation' as the nurse had said. In the morning, a doctor with bad breath and acne had come and shone a little torch into her eyes and told her she was free to go home. The nurse had called her a taxi, but the detective and a WPC were coming in as she was going out and they had kindly driven her home. That had been lucky. But now, sitting in her own front room with a cup of tea and a custard cream, she was finding it very hard to remember exactly what had happened the previous night.

The detective cleared his throat. 'Did the man in the doorway, the one wearing the Che Guevara T-shirt, come right into the shop?'

'It wasn't *him* I was watching,' Mrs Gupta said irritably. She knew it wasn't very gracious of her, but she did wish the two of them would just go away and leave her

2

in peace. Then she could have a nap on the sofa until she felt better.

'Why don't I get you another cup of tea?' It was the WPC who said this. She took the cup out of her hands without waiting for an answer. 'I'll put some extra sugar in.' The WPC seemed nice. The sort of daughter Mrs Gupta wished she had.

'Thank you,' she said automatically. The importance of good manners had been instilled in her from birth. Suddenly she sat up straighter. 'Of course!' Something clicked in her brain, a cogwheel had unjammed. Her eyes brightened. 'Now I remember. How could I have forgotten?' Her eyes met the detective's.

'Yes?' he prompted.

'Snow White went to the fresh fruit section and picked up an apple.'

'An apple.' His voice was flat with disappointment.

'Several apples actually. She picked up a green one first. Then she put it back and picked up a red one. And then another green one. Or maybe it was the same green one for a second time?' She scratched her scalp as she tried to conjure up the precise details. 'And then a red one again. You see, I was watching her in case she slipped something into her pocket. Kids will try anything these days. Anyway, she stared at this red one for ages and then she turned, did another pirouette and walked over towards me. "Hello, my dear," I said. "Is that all you want?" And do you know what she said?' Mrs Gupta paused, waiting for a response.

'No, I don't,' the man said.

'She said, "This apple is poisoned."'

'Really?'

She felt a flash of irritation. Did he not believe her? 'It was just like the story, as if she really believed she was Snow White. She said, "If I eat it, I'll fall asleep and I'll never wake up."' Mrs Gupta paused, but the detective merely nodded. 'And do you know what she did then? She screamed at the top of her voice. Not a word, just a long, ear-splitting yell.'

'And what then?'

'Well, of course, I told her to jolly well stop it. I said if she didn't want the apple, then she should give it to me and go home with her father.'

The detective leant forward, so close that she could smell the pungent scent of stale cigarette smoke through his cheap aftershave. 'Where was her father?' he asked.

Mrs Gupta shook her head. 'I don't know. I looked around but I couldn't see him. He wasn't at the door anymore.'

'What did the girl do after she screamed?'

The detective's questions were endless and Mrs Gupta's head was throbbing. She wished he and the WPC would go away. Trying to remember was making her headache worse. The girl had screamed again. That's right. Twice, in fact. Then she had started twirling round and round and round. Then the girl gave Mrs Gupta a horrid look, and bit into the apple. And then she starting chanting, 'Witch! Witch! Witch!' before running off out of the shop. The apple was in her hand and she hadn't paid.

'Of course, I chased after her. I won't have thieving in my shop. But she was much too fast and by the time I got to the door, she had gone. There was a car driving off. I bet she was in it. Right at that moment I saw Miss Rogers standing on the far pavement. She must have just come back from her father. So I crossed over the road to tell her what had happened, and that was when the shop exploded and I was thrown flat on my face. It was awful. Boom! Just like you see on TV.'

She shut her eyes, and waited for the pain in her head to ease, but it didn't.

'Here's some tea,' the nice WPC said.

Mrs Gupta opened her eyes reluctantly, and took the cup and saucer, cradling them on her lap. 'I've got such a headache.'

'I've almost finished,' the man said. 'Just one more question. Do you think you could describe the father for me? I don't mean his clothes. I mean his face. Imagine he came into your shop dressed in a suit like mine, for example. How would you recognise him? Or maybe you wouldn't. Sometimes when people go through a trauma like you have, they just don't remember.'

Mrs Gupta snapped. 'Of course I'd recognise him. Do you think I'm stupid or gaga, just because I'm old? The man had a tattoo on his neck. I couldn't see what of, but it was all over the side of his neck. He was very tall. And his nose was bent, like it had been broken in the past. And he was as bald as a coot. So why wouldn't I recognise him? I tell you the moment I set eyes on him I knew he was a bad man.'

'Thank you,' the detective constable said. 'You've been very helpful."

Mrs Gupta took a sip of tea. Then she put her cup and saucer down on the glass-topped coffee table and leant back on the sofa. She just needed to shut her eyes and go to sleep. She was sure that when she woke up, the headache would be gone and she'd feel better.

'Can you see yourselves out?' she said.

'Of course,' the WPC said. Mrs Gupta opened her eyes briefly. The two of them were standing in front of her. They glanced at each other, then back at her. Mrs Gupta smiled at them. They had been so kind. They were both so smartly turned out, she in her uniform and him in his suit. And they were both wearing matching black leather gloves. The WPC bent down towards her. There was a cushion in her hands, the big one from the armchair.

'Is that for me?' she said. 'How kind.'

It was and it wasn't. Because the kind WPC pressed the cushion over her face and held it there. For a number of seconds, the old woman's arms thrashed madly. Then, with surprising suddenness, they stopped, frozen briefly in mid-air before flopping down. When the policewoman removed the cushion, Mrs Gupta looked as if she had fallen into a deep sleep.

CHAPTER TWO

When Maggie Rogers woke, her head was drumming with a hangover. For several minutes she lay on her back, staring at the ceiling and unable to move. It had been four a.m. when she finally went to bed, so it was no surprise that there was daylight streaming through her flimsy curtains. She fumbled for her mobile. It was almost midday and the explosion in the shop seemed an age away, an improbable bad dream. Except it wasn't either of those things. What on earth was she going to do? She had hoped that after a few hours of oblivion, things would become clearer and make some sort of sense. But it was quite the opposite. Closing her eyes had brought not peace, but disturbing dreams pockmarked with wild, long-buried memories. She rolled over to the edge of the bed, heaved herself onto her feet and staggered through to the kitchen. It wasn't much of a journey. Her flat had barely enough room to seat a cat, let alone swing one. She removed a mug from the cupboard, filled it to the brim with water and downed it in one. She had consumed the best part of a bottle of white wine on her return to the flat, but the throbbing in her head wasn't, she reckoned, so much a punishment for that as the consequence of stress. She scrabbled around in her handbag, located some paracetamol and swallowed three capsules with another mug of water.

An hour later, she rose from her bed again. This time she showered and dressed — flesh-coloured pants and bra, a pair of jeans, trainers and a purple cheese-cloth top designed to hang down over her thighs and hide a multitude of physical imperfections. Normally she couldn't stop eating, but today her appetite had gone walkabout. She made herself a strong cup of tea and forced herself to take the last banana from the white plate that was currently acting as her fruit bowl. She peeled back the blackened skin, took a reluctant bite and switched on the TV. The Chancellor of the Exchequer was on screen. She shut her eyes, hoping that the noise would drown out her thoughts, until the posh voice was replaced by the nasal tones of the broadcaster moving onto a new story. The words 'fire-bombing of a shop' jumped out at her. She opened her eyes and sat forward. 'Let's go straight to the press conference,' she heard, and instantly they did. A uniformed policeman and a man in a dark suit were sitting side by side behind a table. The uniformed guy introduced himself and uttered several platitudes before passing the mike to the guy in the suit, who had chosen exactly the wrong moment to take a sip of water from the glass in front of him. Detective Inspector Reid — for that was how he was introduced — spluttered, and went red in the face. There was a long pause while he had a coughing fit. Eventually, trying hard not to look embarrassed, he started to speak. He, like his colleague, dealt only in banalities: there is nothing to be alarmed about, we are jumping to no conclusions at this stage, we are pursuing various lines of enquiry and so on, *ad nauseam*. Even Maggie felt her brain glazing over and she had a very personal interest in the case. If the news presenter had been hoping for a dramatic revelation, there wasn't any sign of one so far. Eventually DI Reid dribbled to a halt.

'Can I just ask a question?' There was a pause while the camera found the speaker. His voice was flat and grating. 'My sources tell me that your main line of enquiry is that the attack was racially motivated.'

Reid's face came back into view. He was looking more comfortable now. 'All I can say at this stage is that we are pursuing various lines of enquiry.'

'So you're not denying it then?' the reporter said.

'I am not denying or admitting anything.' He leant forward slightly, looking straight into the camera. 'All I will say is that I urge anyone who was in the vicinity of the incident between eight and nine p.m. last night to please come forward and give us a witness statement. Any information, however trivial, could be important.'

Reid and his superior stood up and left the room and the broadcast returned to the studio. Maggie killed the TV with the remote and pushed the last of the banana into her mouth, gagging slightly on the overripe taste. She took a pull at her lukewarm tea and screwed up her face in thought.

She was still trying — and mostly failing — to think when five minutes later the doorbell rang. She wasn't expecting anyone, so when she opened the front door she was neither surprised nor unsurprised to find a vaguely familiar figure on her doorstep.

'Detective Constable West,' the woman said, as if they had never met.

'Of course,' Maggie said. It was the detective who had asked her a few brief questions the night before, in the street opposite the devastated shop. She was middle-aged, with a snub nose, sunken eyes and a grey bob of hair. The previous night she had been sporting a dark green outfit that was long out of fashion. She was still wearing it.

Maggie invited her in. 'Cup of tea?'

West shook her head. The encouraging smile that had been sewn onto her face the previous night was nowhere to be seen. She seemed embarrassed to be there. The cosy voice had gone too. 'I'd like you to put your coat on and come down to the station with me, dear,' she said. 'If you don't mind.' She said this pleasantly, but her tone suggested that Maggie didn't actually have any choice in the matter. Old-fashioned and school-marmish — like her fashion sense. Maggie knocked back the rest of her tea and scrambled around for her snakeskin-print parka. 'Is it likely to take long?' she asked.

West's mouth twitched. 'Let's go,' she said.

* * *

On arrival at the police station West showed her into an empty interview room. 'Some of my colleagues want to ask you a few questions,' she said and disappeared, shutting the door behind her. Maggie sat down and took stock of the room — a small rectangular table in the centre, four functional chairs, recording equipment on the table to her left, CCTV camera high on the wall. No windows.

There was a noise at the door, but when it opened, it wasn't West who came in. 'I am Detective Inspector Reid and this is Detective Sergeant Ashcroft.' The man making the introductions had closely cropped grey hair, a dark blue suit and eyes that peered warily from under bushy eyebrows. Maggie recognised him from the TV press conference. He placed a cup of tea on the table, sat down opposite her and opened a red folder. Ashcroft — dark grey suit, white shirt, no tie and face like a bulldog — sat down next to him and stared at her.

'I've been reading your statement,' Reid said.

Maggie wasn't sure how to respond, so she sipped her tea and said nothing. Not having something to say wasn't her usual style, but then these weren't usual circumstances.

'An interesting account,' he said, though it was clear from the stress he laid on the word 'interesting' that he wasn't being entirely complimentary.

'What do you mean?' she said, rising to the bait.

He gave a deep breath and turned to his colleague. 'How shall I put it, Sergeant? It seems . . . partial?'

'Load of bollocks, I'd call it, sir.' The sergeant laughed. They both laughed, like two drinking mates in a pub. But when they turned to look at Maggie, the laughter was nowhere to be seen. You're a lying bitch, their faces said.

Maggie shivered involuntarily. Forget Ashcroft's bulldog face, it was more like being in a room with a Rottweiler and a Doberman. She knew her rights, of course, and for a moment she was tempted to demand a solicitor, but she wasn't someone who liked to cave in. Life had taught her that if you lay down on the ground and said sorry, all that happened was that someone stamped on you harder. It was better to play the dumb innocent until she knew a bit more.

So she leant back and smiled at both of them. 'I don't recall making a statement.'

'You spoke to Detective Constable West last night.'

'That's not what I would call a statement.'

Reid leant forward. His right hand began to beat an erratic tattoo on the table. 'Did you speak to Mrs Gupta after the explosion? Yes or no?'

The vehemence of the question took her by surprise. 'Sort of,' she said eventually.

'Sort of? What do you mean by that?'

'She was in shock. Not exactly in a mood to chat.'

'Have you spoken to her today?'

Immediately, Maggie felt guilty. She ought to have rung the hospital at least. She ought to have popped in to see how Mrs Gupta was. She really should have. But what with oversleeping and the detective constable turning up without warning, she hadn't had a chance to do so.

'I'll go and visit her when I'm finished here,' she said as breezily as she could.

'No you won't,' said the Doberman. She turned. Ashcroft's shaven bullet head was thrust forward towards her. She could almost see the slobber dripping from his teeth. 'Didn't you know, darling? Mrs Gupta is dead.'

Maggie's stomach turned a somersault. She thought for a moment that she was going to be sick, but the wave of nausea swept through her and then was gone.

'You mean she died in hospital?' Neither of the men replied. Maggie blundered on. 'She seemed to be all right, apart from a few cuts. The paramedic said she was in shock. That was all.'

'Actually, she died at home.' It was Reid's turn. His voice was softer than Ashcroft's. Perhaps he was more of a bloodhound. He had that drooping face and lugubrious eyes. Maggie wanted to ask about it. She wanted to know how on earth it was that Mrs Gupta had been released from hospital and yet died soon after. How could the doctors have sent her home? What was it she had died of? But even as she was framing these questions in her head, Reid was pushing on. The problem, he was saying, was that Mrs Gupta had died before they'd had a chance to question her. 'So what we need to know, if you don't mind, Ms Rogers, is everything that Mrs Gupta told you.'

'She didn't really tell me anything. I was just comforting her as we waited for the paramedics.'

But Reid seemed unimpressed. He cut in. 'To return to your statement to Detective Constable West, you specifically referred to having had a conversation with Mrs Gupta just after the incident. A *conversation*. DC West was very clear about that. You must have asked her questions. She must have given you answers.'

Maggie shivered. The bloodhound wasn't as dopey as he looked. She took another sip of tea while she considered what to say. Silence was one option, but she didn't think that would work with Reid. She needed to say something that would satisfy him and yet keep him off the scent. 'It was more a monologue than a conversation.' She spoke slowly, weighing her words with care. 'Like I said, Mrs Gupta was in shock. I tried to keep talking to her until the paramedics came. I knew I had to keep her awake, like you're meant to do. I thought maybe she'd banged her head when she fell. You see, I had popped out for a short while—'

'Why was that?' Reid interrupted. 'When I read your statement, my first thought was this: does Maggie Rogers normally "pop out" during working hours, leaving a pensioner in charge of the shop?'

Maggie flinched. She was tempted to give him a lecture on ageism, but she knew that wouldn't help. But she wasn't prepared to back off. She leant forward so that her face and his were uncomfortably close. He smelled of stale sweat and instant coffee.

'I have a friend,' she lied. Not entirely a lie, but enough of one. 'He is much older than me. In his sixties. Just a friend. He used to come to the café sometimes. He took a shine to me. Chatted me up. Brought me flowers. It seemed harmless. He asked me out to the cinema, for a meal. He even took me up to London for a matinee.'

'What did you see?' Reid asked the question casually, as you might when catching up with a friend, but she didn't think he was a casual sort of detective.

'War Horse.'

'Expensive.'

'He paid.'

'So you went to see this guy because . . . ?'

'He has dementia. It's been getting worse for a while, so I try to ring him every evening. But yesterday he didn't answer, so I thought I'd just nip round and see if he was OK and remind him to take his medicine. It was very quiet in the shop. Mrs Gupta is perfectly competent. He's only a five-minute walk away, so there didn't seem a reason not to.' She paused, but only to get her breath. 'His mobile was out of battery, so I plugged it in to recharge it and then I headed straight back. I was just about to cross the road when I saw Mrs Gupta come out of the shop. She looked agitated. When she saw me she started to hurry across the road towards me. And that was when the shop exploded. She fell over, so I helped her up and tried to calm her down.'

She said much of this while staring at her hands. When she raised her eyes, she saw that both detectives were studying her. 'What did she say to you, exactly?' Reid was like a dog with a bone, asking the same question in endless different ways until he got an answer that satisfied him.

Maggie shrugged. 'She wasn't very coherent. It was hard to know what she was saying.'

Ashcroft, the Rottweiler, joined in, baring his teeth. 'Something must have happened to cause her to come out of the shop,' he snarled. 'What was it?''

Maggie considered her options. What was it safe to say? She needed to throw them a morsel, a bone which the two of them could chew on or fight over. 'A girl in a Snow White costume had stolen an apple. She had come into the shop, picked up an apple from the fresh produce area and then taken a bite out of it and run off.'

'And?'

'That was it. That was all she could talk about, the girl dressed as Snow White and the explosion. How loud it was. How frightened she was.'

DS Ashcroft made a noise that sounded like a growl. 'We don't believe you, darling.'

Maggie glared back at him. She wasn't going to be bullied by any man and certainly not by one who called her "darling." 'That's your problem, Sergeant.'

Ashcroft growled another question, 'I'd still like to know why you visited this man during a work shift. Couldn't you have gone afterwards?' Ashcroft had the bone now.

Maggie tried not to react. Dogs can always sense fear. 'I told you. He wasn't answering the phone,' she said deliberately. 'That was unusual. I was worried about him. That's why.'

Ashcroft bared his uneven teeth. 'Very fortunate for you, darling, to be out of the shop when the bomb went off. Convenient even. A more sceptical person than me might come to the conclusion that you were out of the shop because you knew that there was going to be an explosion.'

Maggie felt anger flare. She stood up. 'Do you think I would have gone and left Mrs Gupta in the shop if I was expecting it to be fire-bombed? What sort of person do you take me for?'

'It was merely an observation,' Reid interrupted quickly.

'No, it damned well wasn't. And I'm not going to answer any more questions without a solicitor present.'

Ashcroft growled. He hadn't finished. He snapped. 'Tell us the name of your *War Horse* chum, darling.'

She eyeballed him. 'What, so that you can go round and badger him with a load of questions he won't understand?'

'So that he can confirm that you visited him.'

'He's got no short-term memory. So there wouldn't be much point. He'd just get alarmed.'

'We need his name and address!' Ashcroft slapped his hand down on the table.

Maggie laughed, and waited for Ashcroft to get even angrier.

Reid placed a restraining hand on his colleague's arm. He took over, speaking softly, his face indicating empathy and reason. 'It'll make life so much simpler if you give us the name and address.'

She shrugged. 'I don't see what it has got to do with the explosion. I went out. I came back. I am not denying that. I got cut by some of the flying glass. What the hell has any of that got to do with me visiting a man with dementia? So I will say it just one more time. I'm not answering any more of your questions until I've spoken to a solicitor.'

Reid stood up sharply, his chair scraping discordantly against the floor. 'That won't be necessary. We've finished with our questions, for now at any rate.'

'Well, I've got one for you.' She wasn't going to let the opportunity slip by. 'What makes you think the attack was racially motivated?' she demanded.

Reid's overgrown eyebrows quivered. 'You saw the press conference, did you?'

She nodded.

'Then you'll recall that I neither agreed nor disagreed with the journalist who suggested it.'

'But you think it was?'

He seemed to both smile and frown at the same time. 'The shop is, as you know, owned by a Mr Patel. The press may choose to speculate about motive, but my mind remains one hundred per cent open to all possibilities.'

* * *

Maggie Rogers slipped the key into the lock, opened the door and called out: 'Hi, Dad!' She always called out nowadays. In the past she would ring the bell and wait for him to let her in, but things were different now. If he was watching TV or staring at the wall, wrapped up in his own thoughts, he didn't always respond to the bell. But letting herself in without calling out a greeting or warning seemed impolite to her. She might be his daughter, but it was his flat after all, not hers. She advanced along the corridor and entered the living room. He was sitting on the sofa. He turned and smiled. 'Hello, dear.'

'Hello there.'

The smile on his face faded, and was replaced by a puzzled frown. 'Oh,' he said, with disappointment in his voice. 'I thought you were Peggy. I thought . . .' His words

16

ground to a halt, but even so they were like a punch to Maggie's solar plexus.

She dredged up her cheerful mask. 'She's dead. You know that. Mum is dead.'

Her father didn't reply. It wasn't the first time this had happened. He had said something similar the previous Thursday and it had been such a shock that Maggie had gone home determined to contact the doctor the very next day. Only she hadn't. By the following morning she was telling herself that maybe it had just been a one-off, a case of him having had a bad day. So she had delayed making an appointment. He hadn't made that same mistake on any of her visits since, so she had begun to think of it as just one of those things. She continued to tell herself that reporting it to the doctor would make it official. Then they would test him and analyse him, and before you knew it, her father would be classified as having dementia when all that was happening was that he was getting a wee bit forgetful. Actually it was more than a wee bit. Twice she had come home to find the gas ring turned on and no saucepan anywhere near it. She ought to do something about it.

Arthur, her father, had returned his attention to the magazine that was in his lap. Maggie watched him. He was looking at the pages, but was he actually reading them? Was he taking in any of the words? Did he recognise the photo of that comedian in the middle of the right-hand page?

Maggie went through to the kitchen and switched on the kettle. She stood there, lost in her own world. Why hadn't she just admitted to the police that she had gone to see her father? They would find out in the end if they were half competent. It was easy to tell a small lie. 'I went to see a friend.' And then another little lie and then another. Except that much of what she had said had been true. They had been to *War Horse* in London. They did go out for meals sometimes (though not recently). He was in his sixties. And he had got some form of dementia, maybe Alzheimer's. She now knew that with frightening certainty. It was strange how talking to the detectives had crystallised it. She wondered if they would call her in for further questions with a solicitor present. And if so, how soon? Perhaps they would wait until they had a full forensics report on the shop and the explosion. Perhaps she had a few days' grace — a few days to make and implement a plan.

She made a cup of tea for each of them and returned to the living room, placing his mug on the table beside the sofa. She noticed that he hadn't turned the pages of the television magazine at all because there was still the photo of that wretchedly egocentric comedian there. Then she realised that he had got it open at the previous day's programmes.

'Thank you, Peggy dear,' he said without looking at her. Maggie's stomach lurched again and for a moment she thought she was going to vomit. Her father picked up the mug, took a sip and smiled. 'Just right, my dear. You always could make a good cup of tea.'

* * *

DI Reid could feel the sweat pooling in his armpits. He knew that if he took his jacket off there'd be two embarrassing damp patches on his shirt. It wasn't that it was particularly warm. This office, unlike his own, was air-conditioned. The source of his discomfort was the man sitting across the desk from him, Bill Bowman. Half shut your eyes and he became a Billy Bunter with a fat round face, black-rimmed spectacles and crumpled white shirt. That was what Ashcroft sometimes called him, Billy Bunter or the Fat Owl, when Reid and he were in the car together. But never in the office and never down the pub with the lads. Even Ashcroft wasn't so stupid as to risk career suicide like that. Reid opened his eyes and Billy Bunter became Bill Bowman, the fat bastard. The crumpled shirt was immaculately ironed and the eyes behind the pebble lenses were those of a hawk — or a vulture. He was, Reid knew, some fifteen years younger than him and yet he had already risen higher up the greasy pole than Reid ever would. In fact, Reid suspected that he might soon be slithering back down, unable to hold on to the modest rank he had managed to achieve, while Bowman soared into the stratosphere.

'Not good,' Bowman was saying. His voice was high and squeaky, like Bunter's, but that was where the similarities ended. 'Not good at all.'

The room fell silent. Bowman's bulbous hands were steepled together as if in prayer, which was the last thing Reid could imagine him doing. Bowman picked up the glass of water in front of him and took a sip.

'We're making progress,' Reid said. It sounded feeble.

Bowman laughed. Reid flinched. It wasn't funny. Nothing was funny about being interrogated in the fat man's office. Reid didn't report to him normally. He had only been summoned there once before and that was an experience he wished he could expunge from his memory. So why had he been summoned now? Why was Bowman so interested in this particular case?

'Our key witness is dead, Inspector. She died before you got round to asking her any questions. Is that correct?'

Reid licked his lips. 'Yes, sir.'

'Whereas two unknown persons masquerading as police picked her up from the hospital, drove her home, gave her a cup of tea and presumably asked her a lot of questions before she so inconveniently died. Is that right?'

Reid nodded. 'That is our current assumption.' He could hardly deny it. Less than an hour previously Ashcroft had spoken to the auxiliary nurse who had escorted Mrs Gupta to the hospital doors and passed her into the care of a man in a suit and a woman in uniform.

'Cause of death?'

'We expect to get the results of the post-mortem later this afternoon.'

'Waste of time,' snapped Bowman. 'If it's natural causes, I'm from Azerbaijan.'

'We have a scene-of-crime team going over the old woman's flat. There may be something . . .'

'Another waste of time. These people are professionals. They aren't going to leave cigarettes lying around, impregnated with their DNA. They aren't morons.' He didn't say "unlike you," though Reid had no doubt that was what he meant.

'I'd like to put a 24/7 watch on Miss Rogers,' Reid said.

'Expensive,' Bowman said. Reid waited. He knew the game. If it was important enough, the money would be found. He was pretty certain that for Bowman it was extremely important, though he wasn't sure why. Eventually Bowman gave another laugh, short and sharp. 'It's your call, Inspector.' Then he picked up the phone. Reid stood up. It was his cue to get the hell out of there. He withdrew to the door and opened it.

'Last chance saloon,' the squeaky voice said. Reid pretended not to have heard. He shut the door softly behind him.

* * *

The girl sat on the edge of the bed and stared at the TV. *Bambi* was her second favourite film ever. She wiped her eyes. Bambi's mother had just been shot. It was so sad that she felt her heart would burst, except that she knew things would get better from now on. Bambi would meet Thumper and make friends and grow up and everything would be alright in the end. Except that it wouldn't because Bambi's mother would never come back.

She liked this hotel. It was the fourth one in four days and it was definitely the best. The last one had been a bit stinky. Even Sam had said it was 'crap,' and if Sam had

20

noticed, it had to be true. But this one was a huge room, and her bed was soft and cuddly with pure white sheets and a duvet and three pillows with little red flowers on them. On top there was a dark red bedspread that was silky and shiny. There were lots of posh-looking plastic bottles in the bathroom. When Bambi was finished, she was going to have a bath with lots of bubbles and pretend she was in heaven. She would wash her hair until it was silky, and afterwards she was going to rub the moisturising cream all over her legs and arms and tummy like ladies did. Then she would brush her teeth before she went to sleep because Mummy was sitting up there in heaven watching to see that she didn't forget.

CHAPTER THREE

It was amazing how a good night's sleep cleared the head. After the trauma of the explosion and the disturbed and very late night which followed it, not to mention being interviewed by the police, Maggie Rogers had slept like a log. It was unusual for her to be woken by the alarm. She was a lark, awake by six thirty or so most mornings and temperamentally incapable of lying in bed for longer. Once she was awake she had to get up, and it wasn't just because of her bladder. She fumbled for her mobile and was surprised to see that it was seven twenty-six. The heavy languor of the previous day had disappeared. She showered and dressed with a metaphorical spring in her step and a medley of Abba songs on her lips. There was nothing like a good blast of *Mamma Mia* to get the day off to a good start. By seven forty-five she was sitting at her small circular table with a cup of strong tea, a coconut bar and a fully functioning brain. And now, as well as the host of questions whirling round inside her skull, she also had a few answers.

She hadn't told DI Reid the truth, the whole truth and nothing but the truth. Of course she hadn't. Who did when they were interviewed by the police? When he had asked her about Mrs Gupta, it wasn't that she had lied exactly. It was more that there were things she had omitted to say. She had told him about the girl dressed as Snow White, but she hadn't mentioned the tall skinny guy that Mrs Gupta had talked about. 'He had this ridiculous tattoo all down the side of his neck,' the poor woman had said, 'and he had a boxer's nose, like someone had punched him and broken it.' It was the nose that had convinced her. That, surely, had to be Sam. Who else could it be? The tattoo had initially thrown her off course, but the more she thought about it the more Sam-like the guy seemed to be.

And the girl must be Beth, his daughter. Or rather, Ellie's daughter, and *maybe* his. Ellie had always claimed Sam was the father, but Maggie had had her doubts at the time. Ellie had sometimes been a bit too free with her love in those days. But if the girl was Beth, where on earth was Ellie and why had Sam brought her to the shop? Even Sam wouldn't have knowingly put his daughter in danger — unless of course he was off his head or, alternatively, he hadn't been aware of the risk. Maggie took a slug of tea and bit into the coconut bar. Sam must have come to the shop because he was trying to get back in touch with her. And that could only be bad news. Because getting in touch was the one thing they had sworn they would never do.

She stood up and walked through to the living room. Outside, the sky was dark with cloud and a fine rain spattered against the window, but Maggie's mind was elsewhere. Sam would try and contact her again, she was pretty damned sure. So she needed to have a plan in place. It was as simple as that.

Her own plan preoccupied her as she brushed her teeth and finalised her clothing, and it started to emerge more clearly as she made her way to Hairdelicious. For, as her smartphone had reminded her halfway through her meagre breakfast, she had a hair appointment booked for nine thirty. After that she had her usual shift at Nico's Café, starting at eleven.

* * *

Beth was sitting on the floor, leaning back against the sofa. She was reading *The Lion, the Witch and the Wardrobe* — 'my favourite book ever.' A few weeks previously Sam had read it to her, one chapter each night, from beginning to end, but now she was reading it for herself. She wished the hotel wardrobe was full of fur coats and that she could go into it like Lucy and escape into a magical world. But, of course, the wardrobe had been empty. Hotel wardrobes were always empty.

She looked up. Sam was watching her. He was sitting very still on his bed. Sam could sit or stand stiller than anyone she had ever known. Like a statue, except that every so often his eyes would blink. She was in the middle of a chapter. The faun, Mr Tumnus, had gone missing and she didn't want to stop even for a moment, so she gave Sam a little wave, like the Queen does when she smiles at the crowds from her golden carriage. Then she started to read again. Only when she had got to the end of the chapter did she shut the book and look up again, but Sam was no longer watching her. He had moved over to the window. He was standing to one side and holding the curtain open very slightly while he looked out.

'This is a nice hotel,' Beth said.

'Is it?' Sam's attention was still fixed on the view outside.

'Yes,' she said. She was beginning to get fed up with packing every morning and unpacking every night. She would have liked to stay in one place for a while. 'Can we stay here for another night?'

'We have to keep moving,' Sam said.

'Why?'

'So they can't find us.'

'So who can't find us?'

'The people who are looking for us,' he said. He let the curtain fall back, but walked over to the other side of the window, where he again stared down into the street below.

'What will they do if they find us?' She felt scared suddenly. They must be bad people. She wished Mummy wasn't dead. She wished she was back home.

'You need to get out of those clothes,' Sam said, out of the corner of his mouth.

Beth shrugged and stood up. She twirled around. She was wearing her Snow White outfit, complete with black wig and red bow. Sam had told her that she could only wear her Snow White clothes in the hotel room. She would like to be Snow White all day, to go to a McDonalds and the cinema dressed as Snow White and see people look at her, but Sam said it wouldn't be safe. He said that the people who were after them were looking for a girl dressed as Snow White. Beth wasn't sure if this was Sam being a bit mad. No one would be looking for a girl with a torrent of orange hair, he said. Beth liked it when he called her hair a torrent. It sounded so exotic. Her mother had called it a torrent too. But at school she had been called carrot head, so she didn't like her red hair that much. She would prefer to wear a nice black wig with a red bow. No one would tease her for that.

She picked up the remote and turned on the TV. She flicked through the channels, eventually coming across a Tom and Jerry cartoon. Not as good as Disney, but she liked the way Jerry was always outwitting Tom. For nearly ten minutes she watched intently. Then she realised that Sam was talking on his mobile. Or rather he was shouting into it. He saw her watching him and waved a hand in apology. He walked across the room past her and into the bathroom. He slammed the door. She could still hear him, but it didn't worry her. It was what he did. Sometimes he pretended he was talking to someone on the phone and he'd get very loud and very rude. She didn't worry.

25

Mummy had never worried. 'It just Sam talking to his voices,' she used to say. Beth knew that eventually he would stop shouting and put his mobile away and then they'd have to leave the hotel. She sighed and pulled her black wig off. Sam was a bit weird, but she felt safe with him.

* * *

Maggie Rogers looked forward to her visits to the hairdresser. It was an hour of self-indulgence when she didn't have to look after other people — customers in the shop or restaurant, or her father — and could give herself up to the ministrations of someone else. Ever since she had first moved to Oxford some four years previously, she had come to the same salon. This wasn't because they were exceptionally good or cheap (though they scored pretty well on both those counts) or even convenient (Maggie had moved three times in those four years). She had struck up an almost immediate rapport with Zoe Fisher, the owner of the salon. The very first time had been the clincher. Once Maggie's hair had been shampooed, Zoe had ushered her into her revolving chair, gently talked about possible styles and then got on with the resurrection process. Maggie had shut her eyes halfway through and when she opened them at the end she found she had been transformed. It wasn't exactly an ugly duckling to swan scenario, but it was close enough, and when Maggie had walked out of the salon she really did feel like a new woman. And, to cap it all, Zoe had only charged her a tenner. 'I always do an introductory offer to my new clients,' Zoe had said, holding her coat for her. 'I hope you'll come back again,' she added, while brushing some invisible hairs from the coat lapel.

Zoe was a lesbian. Maggie only found that out when they bumped into each other one Monday morning in Oxford's Cornmarket and ended up having lunch together in the covered market. They chatted animatedly and at the end, as they parted, Zoe had kissed her on the cheek and asked if she had anyone special in her life. Maggie was flattered, but she was determinedly heterosexual and she told Zoe so.

'Not to worry!' Zoe had laughed it off. 'But I hope we can still be friends.'

They had stayed friends, meeting intermittently for lunch or maybe to take in a film on a Monday afternoon, that being a day on which neither of them worked. And of course they had carried on meeting once every month or so when Maggie needed a haircut.

'So what do you fancy today?' Zoe had appeared at her shoulder as if my magic.

'Just a couple of inches, please.' Looking in the mirror, Maggie could see the mock disappointment in Zoe's face. It had become something of a running joke that Maggie never tried anything different.

Zoe leant down closer. 'Fancy a change of colour, Maggs? I'll do you a special deal if you like.'

Maggie shook her head. 'Not today.'

Zoe chattered away through the process. Maggie would have liked to shut her eyes and just think, but Zoe wasn't going to allow that, so she gave up.

It was at the end, when Maggie was paying, that Zoe reappeared by her side. 'Almost forgot, darling. Another letter came for you.' She handed her an envelope.

Maggie knew who it was from, and she had no need to look at it. She stuffed it into her handbag. "Another letter." Zoe made it sound like a common occurrence, when in fact it had happened only twice before.

'Fancy lunch on Monday, Maggs?' Zoe helped her on with her coat. 'There's a couple of good films on in George Street too.' They moved outside and let the door shut before Zoe took her by the arm. 'Are you OK, Maggs? You've been so silent today.'

'The police questioned me.'

'About the explosion? Why?'

'About why I wasn't in the shop at the time. They think it was suspicious that I wasn't there. They thought I knew what was going to happen.'

'Are you serious?'

'They won't question you. I didn't tell them about you. I don't want to drag you into anything.'

'Drag me into what?' Zoe gripped her friend's arm tighter. 'What are you talking about, Maggs?'

'I told them I was seeing my sugar daddy, who has dementia. Probably they'll find out that it's my dad. I hope they do really, because when they find out I've been playing silly buggers with them, they'll stop looking any further. It won't occur to them that was I actually seeing you.'

They were both silent for several seconds.

Then Maggie gave her friend a quick hug. 'I must go.'

'Would you like to talk about it? I could ring tonight. Or we could meet up.'

'No!' Maggie whispered, but with such urgency that Zoe stepped back a pace. 'It's not safe. To meet or communicate at all.'

Then she walked briskly away, across the pedestrian crossing and down the side street where she had parked her car, unaware of the fact that a red-haired woman in the café next to the hair studio was watching her progress with great interest.

* * *

Maggie didn't open the letter for some time. It lay undisturbed in her handbag as she drove her Vauxhall Astra back to East Oxford, parking near her flat by Florence Park. Then she made her way to the Magic Café. Even though time was tight, she walked unhurriedly, putting off the moment of truth. Nico wouldn't mind if she was a few minutes late for work. Her reliability was something he was always commenting on. Inside the café, she treated herself to a cup of peppermint tea and a piece of organic carrot cake. There were two mothers with toddlers sitting on the sofas at the front, but otherwise it was quiet. She bit into the cake and only then did she remove the envelope from her bag.

For half a minute she studied the address on the envelope. It was Ellie's writing alright, neat and extremely legible and written in aquamarine ink. She had always experimented with her colours, and she had only ever used a biro when that was the only option. Had? Maggie pulled herself up. Why was she thinking in those terms, as if Ellie no longer existed? She shivered. She wasn't a person who felt the cold — she had too much insulation on her body as Ellie had once quipped in one of her rare unkind moments — but nevertheless Maggie shivered.

She picked up the knife she had collected from the cutlery tray and, like a surgeon making a first decisive incision, slit the envelope open. She removed a single sheet of white A4 paper. She glanced around the room. Only one pair of eyes was watching her, and they belonged to the male toddler, who was sucking on a red plastic beaker. She dismissed him and began to read. Unlike Sam, who dealt only in cryptic messages, Ellie had written a proper letter of sorts. *Dear Maggie*, it began. *I am being watched. Haven't said anything. Sam is paranoid enough without me adding to it. But I thought you should know. Love from me.*

Maggie folded it up, slipped it back in the envelope and put it into her bag. She sipped at her tea but barely registered the taste. She pushed the carrot cake, a single bite gone, to the centre of the table.

I am being watched. Of the four words it was 'am' that scared her the most. Not 'may be,' but 'am.' Coming from Ellie and given the past, the words had to be taken extremely seriously. Maggie pulled the envelope out of her bag again and studied the stamp and postmark. It had been posted nearly three weeks ago. And she hadn't wished Maggie a happy birthday.

* * *

29

Elgar wished he was working alone. Then he could be making all the decisions himself. Of course, in the service you were ultimately always responsible to someone else higher up the food chain, but when making tactical decisions it was up to you and you alone. Only afterwards, when you had screwed up, did you have to either explain yourself to Him Upstairs or cover your tracks. Elgar was good at that. When it came to concocting a story, J.K. Rowling had nothing on him.

But on this mission he wasn't working alone. He had been ordered to work with Bridget Malone, aka Bridget the Midget. Not that he ever called her that to her face. Even though she only came up to his shoulder, he had seen enough of her in action to know that it would be very dangerous to cross her. Or try to exclude her from any operational decision. He had no doubt that if it suited her she'd drop him in the shit from the top of the highest tower block, or (if there were no tower blocks available) stick a stiletto between his third and fourth rib without the slightest increase in her heart rate. All of which meant that cutting corners, flying by the seat of his pants or trying to pull rank on her were risky options. A memory bobbed to the surface: it was the first time he had been allowed to help light the fireworks on bonfire night. 'Always light the touch paper at arm's length,' his father had insisted time and time again. 'Then retreat to a safe distance.' It had seemed trite and boring at the time, and yet he now looked back on it as being the best advice his father had ever given. He glanced across at Bridget. He thought of her as a firework, only a thousand times more dangerous, and sadly not a rocket that could be dispatched into the stratosphere, never to return. She was something more insidious — a highly explosive Mine of Serpents maybe, pretty as a picture when first activated before suddenly bursting violently and noisily into life (and maybe death).

'God, this is tedious!' he muttered, unable to bear his own thoughts or the silence any longer. The only sign that

Bridget had heard him was a look of disgust that floated across her face like a passing cloud. She was holding a pair of binoculars to her eyes and scanning methodically and unhurriedly from left to right and back again, like someone watching a game of tennis played with a balloon.

'Be not afraid of going slowly,' Bridget said.

'Be only afraid of standing still,' he replied in a bored voice. Bridget had an unending supply of Chinese proverbs, but this was the one she always trotted out whenever he got restive.

'If you've got any better ideas rattling round inside that tin head of yours, maybe you should share them.' Bridget was up for a fight, it was clear. But when wasn't she?

Elgar shrugged. He had finished his stretching exercises, so he went over to his chair, slumped down into it and shut his eyes. He didn't have any better ideas. Bridget's preferred strategy, boring though it might be, was the best one — for the time being at least. Wait and watch Maggie Rogers until something happened. Either she would make a move or Samuel Foulkes would come looking for her again. Elgar was confident — Elgar had a massive supply of confidence when it came to killing people — that he could dispose of Maggie Rogers whenever he chose to do so. But the neat and tidy disposal of Rogers should not, he had been told, be undertaken without prior approval. Him Upstairs had made that very clear.

Elgar looked across at Bridget again. She was still scanning the street. To be fair to her, Bridget was a pretty shrewd cookie. And they were agreed on one thing: based on what the deceased Mrs Gupta had told them, it was highly probable that it was Foulkes who had come to the shop. The old woman's description of a tattoo had briefly confused them, but the rest of her account had tied in with their own assumptions. As for the girl dressed as Snow White, that theatrical piece of distraction was typical of the man. All anyone would remember was that the girl was dressed as Snow White. They wouldn't be able to provide a meaningful description of the girl and they would barely have noticed him. But it was a dead cert that the girl was the dead woman's daughter. That was the second thing the midget and he were agreed on. The fact that they didn't know exactly what she might look like when she wasn't being a Disney damsel didn't really matter. He was distinctive enough and if he was now towing the girl around, it would only be a matter of time before they tracked him down. As for the girl, she was an unfortunate complication, because once they had Foulkes in their sights, she might have to be taken into account.

Elgar shivered, appalled at his thoughts. The job was the job, but kids were a different kettle of fish. He had said as much to Bridget, but she had given him one of her looks and delivered another of her sayings: 'Loose ends are loose ends, and ends left loose will always trip you up.' He suspected that she had made this one up.

He must have fallen asleep shortly after these ruminations because the next thing he was conscious of was a cloud of perfume. He opened his eyes to find her face looming unpleasantly close. 'Your turn,' she hissed. 'And for your information, I'm pretty sure we aren't the only ones keeping a beady eye on Ms Rogers.'

* * *

Aside from working two evenings a week at the food store — though that was clearly going to be on hold for a while — Maggie Rogers worked four daytime shifts at an Italian coffee shop in the Cowley Road, called Nico's Café for obvious reasons. She much preferred this job. For a start Nico was a nice guy. In addition the hours were more civilised, from eleven in the morning to four in the afternoon, after which she often walked the eight minutes to her father's flat to check on him.

32

Normally Nico allowed her a short break after lunch, once things had quietened down. It was while she was on this break, taken with a cappuccino and a piece of cake, that she first noticed the guy in the baseball cap. She was sitting in the window, enjoying the weak winter sunshine and flicking through a copy of the *Oxford Mail* which a customer had abandoned. She barely needed to glance across the road to register the man's presence. Ever since the explosion, her senses had been on high alert. It was as if time had lurched backwards five years, to the time when being under surveillance had been a part of her life. She had ended up treating it as a bit of a game, deliberately leading her tails a dance until their controllers either decided she was no longer worth bothering with or ran out of budget. She had kept moving, from place to place and job to job, until she was pretty sure she was no longer seen as a threat. She had changed her identity — not so hard with her background — and had eventually moved to her father's town. There she settled for trying to establish what passed for a normal life — a job, a flat and a boyfriend. So far, she had achieved two out of three. The couple of guys she had dated hadn't lasted long enough to earn the title of boyfriends, and latterly she had given up on that front altogether, not least because her father had become an increasing source of worry.

As soon as she finished her shift at four o'clock, she left via the front door. The guy with the baseball cap was still there. Previously he had been standing in the doorway of the 24/7, but now he was sitting on one of the pavement tables outside the coffee bar next door to it, pretending to read a book. She headed east. At the pedestrian crossing near Tesco, she joined several other people crossing the road. Glancing to her right, she got another glimpse of the baseball cap, bobbing along the pavement opposite. Her suspicions were confirmed. She was confident that she could lose him if she wanted to, and for a moment she was tempted to do precisely that.

But she killed the urge stone dead. The last thing she wanted was for him to know that she had clocked him. That was probably the only decent card she had in an otherwise poor hand and she needed to keep it in reserve. Whether it was the police, or someone else altogether, who was shadowing her, she couldn't possibly know. But she did know that she would make her move only when she had decided exactly what she was going to do. But at that moment, as she turned into a small grocery store to pick up some items for her father, she had only the broad (and somewhat fuzzy) outline of a strategy in her head.

* * *

As Sam Foulkes saw it, the problem with modern communication was that it was too traceable. Emails and texts, Twitter and Facebook, Skype and messenger services . . . communication was everywhere and it was instant. But all these were more or less easy to intercept. All that was needed was a geek or two, dedicated to the task of tracking you down, and in two shakes of a lamb's tail you were done for. Sam had got himself a couple of pay-as-you-go mobiles three months previously, when he had been feeling particularly paranoid and was worried that his calls were being monitored but he'd only used them once, to check they worked. Of course, a mobile wasn't any use for contacting Maggie because he didn't know her mobile number and even if he did, they'd very likely have a trace on it. He could ring the café she worked at, but the chances were they'd be listening in on that phone too. He wouldn't put it past the bastards. Walking into her café in disguise and pretending he was a customer was a possibility, but his height made that a risk. So he'd have to resort to old-fashioned methods. He had used the personal ads in the past, but those left a public trail, and if he used a code Maggie would recognise, how could he be sure that they wouldn't work it out too? Whoever *they* were! Sam suddenly put his head in his hands. One of his voices was telling him he was an arsehole, but that familiar voice was harsh and troublesome and he banished it with a volley of swear words.

'Sam!' He turned and saw Beth's eyes on him. 'You know Mummy hates you swearing in front of me.'

He couldn't get used to the way she sometimes spoke as if her mother was still alive and had just gone to the corner shop. Was Beth in denial? Did the memory of Ellie live on in the girl's head? Or did Beth hear Ellie's voice? The thought jolted him. She was still a child. He hadn't heard voices when he was her age. 'Sorry, Beth!' he said, hiding his anxiety with a smile and a playful smack on the back of his own wrist. 'Naughty Sam!'

After that he withdrew into the bathroom and locked the door. But now he was there he had no more swearing to do. He leant over the basin and splashed cold water onto his face. Another voice began to speak. 'Maybe Beth is the answer.' The voice was female and kind and persuasive, a mixture of Ellie and his own mother. It was the only voice he trusted. He stared into the mirror and saw the chaotic hair and the stained T-shirt, and realised that of course Beth *was* the only answer.

* * *

Beth was finding it hard not to burst out laughing. But she knew she mustn't. She needed to keep calm and do exactly as Sam had said so that no one could possibly guess that she was the little Snow White girl who had been in the shop just before it had exploded. She had heard the bang as they hurried away, but Sam had grabbed her hand and told her not to look back, which of course she had. She had seen fire coming out of the door and had wanted to stop and watch, but Sam had dragged her round the corner.

There had been pictures of Snow White on the front page of the newspaper. Not her dressed as Snow White, but the real Snow White from Disney. Sam had been

35

pleased when he saw it. 'That means they haven't got any photos of you, Beth.'

She didn't really understand why he was so pleased. Wouldn't it be nice if she *was* on the front page of the newspaper, or even on TV? Everyone wants to be on TV, don't they? After all, the explosion was nothing to do with them.

Sam was taking a bath. That was unusual. She couldn't remember him having had one for ages. Half the time he didn't even take a shower. Sometimes he'd get very smelly. Tonight, for example, he had smelled worse than a skunk. She had said so and he'd laughed.

'Mummy doesn't like you to smell,' she had told him. 'We're not hippies anymore.' Sam had disappeared into the bathroom. Beth had assumed he was going start shouting into his phone again, so she was really surprised when she heard the taps running. He was definitely filling the bath! Soon the taps were turned off and it all went quiet. He wasn't doing any shouting. She went and stood close to the door. After a while she heard him singing some ancient pop song. 'Hey Jude!' he sang. She giggled, though not at his singing. As she turned away from the door she had seen herself in the dressing-table mirror again. She couldn't believe what Sam had done. It was crazy!

CHAPTER FOUR

Maggie spotted the message while she was eating breakfast. She was studying Ellie's letter again. The anxieties which had welled up in the Magic Café the previous day resurfaced. Unlike Sam, Ellie was not the paranoid type. If she had written to Maggie to tell her she was being followed, then it was very likely that that was the case. But what the hell could Maggie do about it?

She put the letter back and frowned, studying the envelope for clues. The careful script in aquamarine ink, slightly smudged. The first class stamp. The postmark — definitely London, as she would expect.

Maggie turned the envelope over. She smiled. On the back, as always, was a stamp proclaiming Ellie's latest allegiance: 'I love Trident.' She frowned. The last time, on her birthday card envelope, it had been 'Animals have Rights too.' And a couple of years before that, the familiar 'Stop the Bloody War.'

I love Trident? 'To Hell with Trident' would be more like Ellie. Or was it a heavy irony? Maggie felt her throat tighten and her eyes moisten. Why oh why had they ever fallen out?

That was when she spotted it. Half-hidden and camouflaged by the Trident slogan, written in pencil, so lightly inscribed, so faint that even if the slogan had not been there it would have been easy to miss. Maggie lifted the envelope closer to her face and squinted. Six words. Intended for Maggie alone, and no one else.

Maybe I should retire soon?

Was it a joke? Retire? Ellie was only thirty-three or thirty-four. Retire from what? Ellie, like Maggie herself, had trained as a teacher, but neither of them had lasted the pace. The problem was they had both been rebels, more interested in protesting against adults than teaching kids to be obedient. Had been rebels? Or still were? Maggie had suppressed it for nearly five years now, telling herself that marching, living in trees under the threat of destruction or chaining herself to railings were all futile gestures. Governments still went to war, bypasses were still driven through fragile ecosystems and pharmaceutical companies still used animals to test their drugs.

But what about Ellie? Was she retiring from the protest world? Was that it? If she was aware of being under surveillance, maybe she had decided that enough was enough. Beth was growing up and it seemed that Sam had become a semi-permanent fixture in her messy life. Maybe in the circumstances she had decided to give up all that protesting and settle for being an ordinary, boring, law-abiding nine-to-fiver. It made a depressing sort of sense, though somehow Maggie couldn't quite believe it.

* * *

Maggie was serving two steel-haired ladies a skinny latte and a cappuccino when it began. It was eleven thirty in the morning, there was only a scattering of customers and Nico had gone off to the bank.

'Oh my God!' said the one with the dangling earrings.

For a millisecond or two Maggie thought she was referring to the coffee. She knew how rude some customers could be.

But the woman was staring out through the window. She pointed. Smoke was pouring out of the 24/7 shop opposite and Maggie saw two women staggering out, coughing and screaming.

For a big woman Maggie could move fast. She was out of the door before most of the people in the restaurant were even aware of something being wrong. Outside, however, panic had taken hold. A car had pulled up and a Good Samaritan was clambering out to help. But the car behind swerved out and overtook, horns blaring, its driver desperate to put distance between herself and any danger. Maggie coughed as a gust of smoke eddied around her and that was when she realised there was another fire, in the bookshop right next door to her restaurant. The next minute or so was a blur of activity. She charged straight back into the café, bellowing 'fire!' at the top of her voice. She grabbed the woman with the dangly earrings by the upper arm and dragged her outside. Her companion needed no help. Maggie went back into the café. Nico was the boss, but since he was absent she felt responsible. There was no sign of any fire in the restaurant itself and the room was already clear of people. The kitchen area was empty too. She pushed through the swing doors at the back and banged open the two toilet doors. No one there either. Only then did she go back out onto the street, where she bumped into a small boy in a red football shirt and shorts.

'Sorry!' she said.

'Sorry!' the boy replied, and thrust something into her hand. And then he turned and jogged off down the pavement, jigging left and right like a miniature Ryan Giggs. In the distance Maggie heard the sirens of police cars and fire engines. She looked down at her hand and saw a small piece of neatly folded paper. She didn't open it, merely slipped it inside her blouse and down into her bra. She was pretty sure who it was from and she was also damned certain that there was no danger of anyone being burnt alive. She almost laughed out loud. These were smoke bombs, not fire bombs. Sam did confusion and distraction, not death.

* * *

It took an hour for the police to satisfy themselves that there was nothing more to worry about. In the meantime, with the street cordoned off, Nico and Maggie went to another Italian café two streets away. The owner was a friend of Nico's and she insisted on giving them each a glass of wine and a double espresso to counteract the shock. Then she sat down with her own glass of wine and chatted to Nico in animated Italian, which was a blessing for Maggie because she had no desire to talk. When the all-clear came, they returned to Nico's Café and tried to carry on as if nothing had happened. But that was hard to do. For a start, journalists and photographers kept coming into the café, ostensibly for coffees and cakes, but really in the hope of a lurid first-hand account. 'Tell me how it felt?' one guy asked, eyes gleaming. 'Was there a moment when you thought you were going to be burnt to death?'

Maggie played dumb and told him to talk to Nico. The last thing she wanted was to have her words and her photo splashed across the media.

Lunchtime came and went in a whirl of customers in a hurry and by mid-afternoon Maggie was beginning to flag. At four o'clock she said goodbye to Nico as usual and made her way to her father. It was important to maintain a routine. She spent an hour and a half there, making his supper and doing a bit of tidying and cleaning, before heading for home when *Pointless* came on the TV. Often she stayed and watched it with him, but she thought she'd rather watch the news in the privacy of her own flat.

40

As it turned out the story didn't get any coverage. Graphic images from the Syrian civil war, the disappearance of a child up north and the continuing economic crisis all proved more newsworthy, it didn't even make the local news. Smoke bombs that had caused no damage to property or people were not that exciting — unless you had happened to be there at the time.

After watching the news, Maggie cooked herself a supper of leftovers. Various bits of vegetable, some dried-up cheddar and two eggs a day past their sell-by date became an omelette. She removed two slices of bread from the freezer, toasted them and decided to eat one of the two purple yoghurts at the back of the fridge. The other would do for breakfast.

Normally she ate with the TV or the radio on, but tonight she opted for silence. Her plan was coming together in her head. She slipped her hand into her bra and pulled out the piece of paper the boy had given her. She had looked at it already, in the bathroom at her father's flat, so she knew what it said — nothing but a string of numbers. It hadn't been a surprise. In the old days that was how Sam, Ellie and the others had always communicated. There were twenty-two digits. The first twelve made up a map reference — a six-digit x-coordinate and a six-digit y-coordinate. Except that it wasn't quite as straightforward as that. It never had been with Sam. He had always been paranoid about security, so even the twelve digits had to be scrambled. There was no intrinsic logic to it, merely a system which Sam had devised and then drummed into the few of them that needed to know.

The remaining ten digits were a date and time. According to the note, Sam wanted to rendezvous the following day at 19.03. But he didn't mean exactly 19.03, merely round about seven o'clock in the evening. As for the map reference, the easiest thing would have been to enter it into Google Maps, but she wasn't so stupid as to do that. If they weren't monitoring her internet activity by now, then she was the Queen of Sheba. She still had some paper maps and she had dug these out of the drawer at the bottom of the wardrobe. They weren't detailed enough to give her a precise location, but they were enough to take her pretty damned close and that was good enough for her because she knew the area. Sam had met her there once before. It was why he had chosen it. Maybe she'd drop by the library in the morning and double-check on one of the public computers.

* * *

Elgar waited until Bridget was three mouthfuls into her hamburger before he asked her the question that had been bothering him.

'So what do you think that was all about then?'

Bridget raised her eyes so that they momentarily met his, then returned her attention to her food. They were sitting at the back of the joint in the corner, so that they had a good view of everyone coming in and going out. Not that they were expecting anyone significant to come in. It was merely second nature. Always make sure you could see what was going on, that there was no possibility of someone sneaking up behind you and that an exit route was available if required. Elgar had already scouted that out. There was a corridor past the toilets which led out into a small yard at the back.

'Well?' Elgar prompted. His voice was lower than it needed to be. There wasn't anyone within easy earshot and there was some tuneless music blaring overhead. 'You don't set off smoke bombs just for the hell of it, do you?'

Bridget took another bite and continued to ignore him.

'I mean, was it one of them who did it? If so, why? Or if it wasn't one of them, who the hell was it?'

Bridget set the remains of the hamburger down on her napkin and took a long suck of cola via a straw.

'He's got a history of it, hasn't he?' she said, fixing Elgar with an icy stare. 'You've read the background on them, haven't you? He likes messing around with things like that.'

'But there wasn't any point to it.' In a parallel world, Elgar would have been shouting, and very likely shaking her by the shoulders too. But in reality he lowered his head and dropped his voice even further. 'It's not as if she tried to do a runner in the confusion. And we didn't even see him.'

Bridget laughed. It was her dismissive, patronising, what-a-stupid-man laugh. 'He was pissing into the air and hoping we were standing downwind.'

Elgar considered this for several seconds as he wiped his final chip through what remained of the tomato sauce. As well as being extremely unpleasant, Bridget was smart. Not that he would have admitted it to her. That was why he had asked her the question. But somehow this time her answer didn't satisfy him.

'So we just keep watching them, do we, until they do make a move?'

Bridget pushed the last of her hamburger into her mouth and chewed it slowly. Then she wiped her hands and leaned forward again. 'I was thinking,' she said, 'that maybe we should make a move ourselves.'

CHAPTER FIVE

Losing the tail was as easy as ABC. It was the same guy as before, but with different clothes: black leather jacket, navy blue T-shirt, jeans and trainers — an unexceptional merge-into-the-crowd outfit. Watching him from inside Nico's Café, Maggie sensed that he was already getting careless. He rarely looked across. It was hard not to conclude that he was getting used to the idea that she had a fixed routine and that she was unlikely to do a runner. That suited her fine. At half past three, she disappeared into the staff toilet in her black-and-white waitress costume. Four minutes later she emerged, dressed in a brown and white animal print dress, skin-coloured tights, calf-length tan boots and a red weave flat cap. Over this outfit she slipped on a knee-length red trench coat, before hoisting a brown bag over her shoulder and marching out the front door. Even Nico, who had agreed to her leaving half an hour early, seemed not to recognise her as she brushed past him. But that wasn't just because of the radical change of clothes. Maggie Rogers was also now sporting a shoulder-length blonde wig. She swung right, marching boldly along the pavement before cutting left across the zebra crossing. A glance over her shoulder confirmed that leather-jacket man was still sitting with his paperback, sipping his latte as if he hadn't a care in the world. She walked for some thirty seconds before striding across the road between the stationary vehicles. She plunged down Temple Street, then turned left up the Iffley Road, walking as fast as her heels would allow. A couple of times she paused and looked behind her, but there was no sign of her incompetent tail. She began to relax, but not to slow down.

She reckoned she was a bare five minutes from her father's flat. And time was of the essence. She needed to get a start on whoever it was who was watching her before they realised that she had gone AWOL. She needed to get her father into the car, drop him off at St Botolph's and then get the hell out of there before the alarm was raised. She had considered ringing Sister Mary at St Botolph's the night before, but had decided against it. She would just drop him there and go. There was no way Sister Mary would not take him in. And there was no way that she herself could just leave him in his flat on his own now. It wouldn't be safe. She had thought it through. This was the only alternative.

When she got to her father's block of flats, the lift was conveniently on the ground floor. Seconds later she was outside his door. She checked her watch. By her reckoning, she had maybe thirty minutes before her shadow realised she hadn't left the café at the usual time. Maybe a few more minutes while he checked inside and realised she wasn't there. Then the shit would hit the fan. By which time she and her father needed to be long gone.

She slipped her key into the lock. 'Dad!' she called out as usual. He would be in the living room, but she turned first into his bedroom, pulled open the wardrobe and extracted a blue holdall. She had packed it herself the previous evening while he was engrossed in the TV. 'Dad!' she called out again urgently. She did hope he wasn't going to be a trouble and insist he had to finish the TV programme he was watching. He could be such an awkward cuss when the mood was on him. She dropped the holdall in the hall and moved through to the living room, but her father wasn't slumped there on his sofa or indeed anywhere else in the room. She stood still, bewildered. Then she went into the small kitchen. There was no sign of him there either. She went to the bathroom, but the door was open and the tiny space empty.

In all her planning, the one thing that hadn't occurred to her was that he would forsake his afternoon TV and go out. He never went out at this time of day. He was always there when she arrived, waiting for her to make him a cup of tea and then his supper. She went back to the living room and looked around again. She couldn't believe it. He had to be there somewhere. If he had decided to play some childish game of hide and seek, there weren't many places he could easily hide. She went and checked behind the sofa, just in case, but of course he wasn't there. Could he be hiding under the coffee table? The answer, she told herself irritably, was definitely 'no.'

She looked again at her watch and then around the room. And then she saw the envelope, propped neatly against the TV screen. She was surprised she hadn't noticed it when she first entered the room. She walked over and saw with a shock that it had her name on it. The 'Ms Maggie Rogers' was printed, not hand-written. She ripped open the envelope and pulled out a single white sheet of paper. She unfolded it. It too was printed, which ruled out any possibility of it being from her father. She felt herself go cold. Her legs wobbled beneath her. She grabbed the sideboard with her right hand.

We have your father, she read. *He is safe. We will be in touch. Keep our mobile with you at all times.*

Our mobile? For a moment her thoughts were scrambled. What were they talking about? Then she saw it — an unfamiliar handset half-hidden under the TV screen, behind where the letter had been propped, plus a phone charger and another charger for use in the car. Whoever they were, they were leaving nothing to chance. There was no name at the bottom of the letter and certainly no signature.

'Oh God!' she said, not in prayer or supplication, but in horror. She sat down on the arm of the sofa and tried to think. She had assumed that the idiot watching her at the café was from some section of the police, a detective constable working for Reid probably. Another possibility was that it was Special Branch, which was altogether more serious. But even Special Branch would hardly have abducted her father. Or would they? Someone abducted him, someone buried deep in the security services she guessed, and they had done it for a reason. She was that reason. But if they wanted to talk to her, they could have picked her up at any time. Whoever it was that was watching her wanted to see where she went or who she met. Which meant — what?

She could feel panic welling up. There was no doubt now. Her past was catching up with her. But not just with her, with her father too. Another emotion swept through her now, anger. How dare they involve him! Who the hell did they think they were? He was an old man, innocent and confused. *Bastards!*

* * *

Arthur Rogers was used to playing the old fool. It was very effective when you were out and wanted help in the supermarket or attention from the waitress in the restaurant. Act a bit gaga and it was remarkable how kind people could be. Latterly, however, things had changed. It had become not so much a case of acting the fool as being one. This had happened quite suddenly. The first time it was as if half the day had been wiped from his memory. He remembered leaving the flat just as the cuckoo clock in his living room chirruped ten o'clock, but after that — nothing. The next thing he knew he was sitting in front of

47

the TV watching *Murder She Wrote*. The front door had opened and Maggie's voice had sung out a cheery greeting. She had come through and flung her coat over the chair. 'That's a nice mug, Dad,' she had said. 'Is it new?' He had looked at the yellow mug in question, sitting half full on the coffee table, and for the life of him he couldn't remember where on earth it had come from.

A thought had flashed through his brain, like a comet across the skies. Perhaps Maggie had begun to suspect something. Recently he had noticed that her face would crease with worry if he didn't respond to a question or couldn't tell her what he had been watching on TV when she asked him. Her visits were becoming more regular now too. He knew that because as soon as she went home he would open up his diary and write the letter 'M' in the top right-hand corner of that day. And then there was all the extra questions she asked him — where had he been that day, what had he been watching on the TV, quizzing him on the news. He didn't like it. He was fond of her, she was the only daughter he had. But she shouldn't try and catch him out. So he had tried to hide his occasional confusion from her. Senility, dementia, Alzheimer's . . . whatever it was he wanted to pretend that it wasn't happening to him.

When the two Jehovah's Witnesses had appeared at his door, he had instantly turned on the senility act. As well as being a means of getting help from people, it was also his protection against unwanted visitors. He hadn't wanted to let them in, but just as he was shutting the door in their faces, the woman had asked him if she could possibly use his toilet. She had such a friendly smile that he hadn't had the heart to refuse.

While she was in the toilet, the man had asked him if he wanted to be saved.

'No,' he had said very firmly. He really didn't want to get into a discussion about that. He'd never get rid of them then.

The man had shrugged. An awkward silence followed. Eventually the woman reappeared from the toilet. She was holding a photograph in her hand, a small one of Maggie at about twenty-five. 'Is this your daughter?'

'You've been in my bedroom!'

'We know this is your daughter,' the woman said.

Arthur felt his chest tighten. 'I'd like you to go,' he had said, but the woman had just smiled.

'We know Maggie Rogers is your daughter.'

That was when he had begun to get scared. How could they possibly know? And who were they? Because they sure as heck weren't Jehovah's Witnesses. So Arthur had retreated into senility. When they said he would have to come with them, he had thought of resisting or shouting, but the look on the man's face convinced him it wouldn't be a good idea. So he had gone along with them without making a fuss and had continued to play the going-gaga card ever since. That way he would be safer and Maggie would be too, because he wasn't so senile that he hadn't realised that it was her they were interested in. He couldn't help but wonder — and worry — if her past might not be catching up with her.

* * *

Sam had met her here once before. A bit more than four years ago, at this very same godforsaken spot. It had been a miserable day in mid-October, rain lashing down, no wind, heavy black cloud. She had waited in the car for several minutes, wondering where the hell he had got to. Then there had been a sudden bang on the passenger window and she had almost jumped out of her skin.

'Unlock the bloody door!' he had shouted. When he had clambered in, he was wetter than the proverbial drowned rat and yet bubbling with excitement. 'Let's get the hell out of here, darling,' he said, 'before the pigs come looking.'

Today it was dry. Still no blue sky, but no sign of rain either. She got out of the car and stretched her back. She was pretty damned sure she hadn't been followed, but she left the driver's door open and the engine running as she scoped the location. It was the sort of lay-by that gives lay-bys a bad name, a crazy jigsaw of holes and ruts, where no sane person would choose to stop. That, of course, was probably its attraction for Sam. There was a dense coppice of bushes and trees that separated it from the main road and screened the car from passing vehicles. She turned a full circle. Where had he got to?

'Hey, doll!' The voice took her back several years.

'Where the hell have you been?'

'This is Beth,' he said, gesturing to the small figure standing by his left leg. 'Only at the moment we are pretending she is Matt. She's very good at pretending.'

'Hi, Beth!' Maggie said, taking in the short hair, red football shirt, jeans and trainers. 'We've met, of course.'

'Matt,' the child said firmly. 'My name is Matt.'

A mobile phone rang. Sam swore.

'It's mine,' Maggie said. It was the phone from her father's flat. That could only be bad. 'Who's calling?' she said.

'Is Sam there?' It was a woman's voice.

'Who's Sam?'

'Don't play silly buggers, Maggie,' the voice said. Sharp and determined. 'We've got your father with us.'

Her stomach somersaulted wildly. Even though she had known this call would come sooner or later, she felt the fear rip through her body. 'I want to speak to him,' she replied as calmly as she could.

'And I want to speak to Sam.' The woman spoke with an Irish accent, strong and angular, definitely not the soft brogue of popular myth.

'You first,' Maggie said, trying to sound more resolute than she felt. 'Or I hang up.'

There was a long pause. Maggie could feel her heart thumping like a drum. Then she heard a male voice. 'Ciao, Maggie.'

'Dad! Are you alright?'

'*Arrivederci*!' And her father giggled like a child who has overdosed on coca cola.

The woman took over. 'Seems like he doesn't want to talk anymore. So let me speak to Sam.'

Sam grabbed the phone and moved away from Maggie, turning his back as if afraid she might try and snatch it back. 'Who the fuck are you?'

There was a laugh. 'No need to be aggressive, Sam. I just want us to meet up and have a chat.'

'Is that what you said to Ellie? Let's have a chat.'

'Where exactly are you?' the voice said.

'Can't you tell, with all your bloody gadgetry?'

'Don't lose your temper with me, Sam, not if you want Maggie to see her father again. I'd like to arrange an exchange.'

'Yeah, I bet you would!'

'I will hand over her father if she hands over you.'

'You must think we were born yesterday.'

Sam glanced across at Maggie as he said this. His face was rigid. His eyes seemed to recede deep within his face. She recognised the look from old. She opened her mouth. She wanted to warn him not to say or do anything rash or stupid, but she was too late. He was holding the mobile away from himself at full stretch and was staring at it as if searching for enlightenment. Then he dropped it on the ground and jabbed the heel of his Doc Marten hard onto it. Once, twice, three times.

* * *

Beth kept her hands over her ears and pretended she couldn't hear them. She was in the back of the car. Sam and the woman were in front. The woman was driving. She had one hand on the steering wheel while she waved

51

the other one around as if she had a crab attached to one of her fingers and was trying to shake it off. She was screaming at Sam. Sam wasn't shouting back, though he was talking pretty loudly. He kept telling the woman, 'Stop shouting and calm down,' but Beth could see that the woman had no intention of doing either of those things. The woman was angry. She was really worried about her father. Beth felt sorry for her.

'They'll kill him!' the woman sobbed. 'If they can't contact me, they'll kill him. They said so. They said if I turned off my mobile even, they'd kill him. And what do you do? You bloody well smash it with your hobnail boots!'

Beth lifted her hands away from her ears a little, so that she could hear better. The woman wasn't going to hurt Sam, she was pretty sure of that. She wasn't shouting quite as loudly now and her hand was tugging at her hair, not waving in the air.

'It won't be just your dad they'll kill, it'll be all of us. You know that.' Sam said this in a very calm voice. Beth recognised it as the one he used after having one of his shouting fits in the bathroom. The calm voice was a good thing.

'They will have been tracking the mobile,' Sam continued. 'For all we know they may be only a few miles away.'

'They said they would kill my father.'

'They won't,' he replied. And then Sam did something very un-Sam-like. He reached out his hand and placed it on the woman's shoulder.

'Stop it,' she said, but Sam's hand didn't move and he continued to talk in his super-calm voice.

'Maggie, your father is a bargaining chip. You know that. Either they will have killed him already or they will keep him alive for as long as they think he is useful.' Sam removed his hand. 'If we had kept the mobile turned on, they would have caught us all. Your dad wouldn't want that. He would want you to live. It's what dads do. They want their kids to live long and happy lives. And if anything threatens their kids, they'll do whatever it takes to protect them. Absolutely anything. I know that only too well.'

'And I know something too,' the woman said. 'You're a bastard.' But at least she wasn't shouting any more. Mind you, Beth thought, it would be a lot safer if she kept her eyes on the road, rather than keep looking at Sam as she drove.

'Shush!' Sam said glancing behind him. 'Remember we've got Matt in the back.'

Beth could have pointed out that she'd heard Sam swear lots of times, but she didn't. She wasn't going to diss Sam in front of this woman. Besides, she was feeling tired. In the front the two adults fell silent. She was relieved to see that the woman now had both hands on the steering wheel. As for Sam, his right hand was resting on the woman's shoulder again. Now that, Beth thought as her eyelids flickered shut, was very odd. Very unlike Sam indeed.

* * *

'I need to spend a penny,' Arthur said. It was the first time he had said anything since they had got into the car, nearly two hours previously.

Elgar, sitting in the back with the old man while Bridget drove, turned to look at him. He had been lost in his own thoughts and for a moment he wondered if he had imagined it. The old man was looking straight ahead, eyes open wide, mouth firmly shut. He looked like he was lost in his own world. Elgar wondered what that world might be. Was it one of confusion and chaos? Where am I? Who am I? Or was it a world of memories? Childhood. First love.

'I don't want to wet my trousers,' the old man said, more loudly.

Bridget swore. 'Can't you wait?'

Arthur didn't reply.

'Just pull up somewhere, for God's sake,' Elgar snapped. It was him sitting next to Arthur, not her. 'Or the whole car will stink of piss.'

He half expected Bridget to snarl back, which was her usual *modus operandi*. She merely gave a gasp of irritation and a flick of her head. She began to slow down.

She pulled into a field entrance with a locked metal barrier across it. Arthur got out and urinated by the barrier, while Bridget slipped under the bar and disappeared behind the hedge. 'Keep an eye on him,' she ordered needlessly. Elgar felt a surge of resentment. Why wouldn't he keep an eye on him? And even if he didn't, what were the chances of the old boy high-tailing it while his back was turned? Nil! As if to prove his point, Arthur clambered back into the car and strapped himself in, a vacant smile on his face.

Elgar took his turn to relieve himself and then began a few stretch exercises. When Bridget reappeared, she leaned against the barrier, allowing the breeze to ruffle her hair. Elgar went and stood next to her. He spoke in lowered tones. 'Maybe kidnapping the old man was a mistake.'

Bridget said nothing. After several seconds he glanced sideways at her. Almost immediately she turned and gave him one of her stares. 'Is that what you think?'

'He's an encumbrance,' he replied.

'He's a card we may need to play,' she said, turning her face back towards the wind.

'He's gaga,' Elgar insisted. 'He'll be pushing up the daisies soon enough anyway, so why would his daughter risk everything to save him?'

'Why?' She gave a hoot of derision. 'That *is* the reason, you idiot,' she continued. 'Because she's his *daughter*. She'll want to save him. She'll capitulate.'

'If we need to move fast, he'll be in the way.'

'If he's in the way, we'll get rid of him.' She spoke slowly, one word at a time, like a teacher explaining something to a particularly stupid schoolboy. He hated it when she did that.

'We could set him free somewhere remote,' he went on. 'Like here. He's never going to remember us.'

Bridget's only reply was the slightest shake of her head. Then she walked over to the car and got in. Elgar shrugged and followed. The lady's not for turning. The expression should have been coined for the hard-nosed bitch he had to work with. Margaret Thatcher was small fry in comparison.

* * *

Maggie waited until she was sure that Beth was fast asleep before asking the question that had been nagging her throughout the day. They had picked up supper from a McDonalds and eaten it in the car. It went against all of Maggie's home-cooked, organic principles, but Sam had insisted and Beth had been so ecstatic that Maggie wondered what Sam normally produced for her. She had been tempted to argue — arguing the toss was something she used to be good at — but exhausted by the previous few days, she was only too ready to let him take charge. Eventually they had stopped at an old-fashioned and somewhat rundown hotel a couple of miles off the motorway, which Sam said he had used before. The woman on reception — late thirties, Maggie guessed, northern accent and breasts to die for — had greeted him as if he were a long lost friend. She had flirted so outrageously with him that Maggie found herself wondering if he and she didn't perhaps know each other from previous visits, biblically speaking even. That would also explain the fact that the blonde (dyed, of course) cow had fixed them up with a large twin-bedded room. Not that Maggie wanted a double — far from it — but the idea was to look like a proper family. As far as Maggie was concerned, parents who weren't so old that they were beyond sex normally slept in one bed. Beth had been allocated her own small single room accessible only through theirs, which ensured the girl's safety. The connecting door of dark stained oak also ensured their privacy, which was a damned good job as far as Maggie was concerned, because there was stuff that they definitely needed to talk about.

'Where's Ellie?' Maggie finally asked after double-checking that Beth was tucked up in her bed. Already she felt responsible for the child.

Sam didn't answer at first. And not at second either. Maggie waited. She knew he had heard her question and past experience had taught her that there wasn't anything to be gained by hassling him. She sat on her bed, facing him, while he rocked steadily on his, eyelids half closed. She was reminded of an elephant she had seen in a wildlife park somewhere in the West Country, swaying rhythmically forwards and backwards in a state of distress. It had been standing in a sunken concrete pen whose gates were wide open. Beyond lay an expanse of green paddock, yet at no stage did the animal attempt to venture out. She had watched mesmerised for at least half an hour, willing the poor creature to escape. The sadness she had felt had been overwhelming. 'Sam?' she prompted.

His head twitched. He opened his mouth, but before he could speak, a door creaked. Maggie turned and saw Beth standing there, little girl lost expression on her face. She blinked at them and gave a little sob.

'Hey, what's up, pet?' Sam held his hands up in front of him in mock surrender. 'Are we being too noisy?'

Beth didn't answer. Her gaze was fixed on Maggie. Maggie had the feeling that she was being examined and found wanting.

Silence. The two adults waited for the child. 'It was a hit-and-run,' Beth said softly. 'Mum was killed by a car.'

More silence. The only noise came from the water pipes. Someone somewhere was running a bath. 'I need to spend a penny,' Beth said.

* * *

It was like being summoned to the headmaster's study for punishment. All six of them called in to answer for their collective misdemeanours. As they trooped in, Reid half expected Bowman to be wearing a gown and to have a cane lying ready for action on his desk. For some reason the image made him feel better. He was even tempted to smile. After all, what more did he have to lose? Early retirement would be a blessing as far as he was concerned. But he didn't think Bowman would let him off that easily. And besides, he had called the whole team in. The silence was as thick as a Victorian smog and the tension was palpable. Even Ashcroft, who fancied himself as a hard man, looked uneasy. He had also, Reid noticed, opted to sit on the far side of the room, as far away from Reid as he could possibly get. Ashcroft's face was redder than usual, with a sheen of sweat. By contrast Evans' was sheet white and there was a good reason for that. Evans was the idiot who had been watching the Rogers woman when she went AWOL. Reid didn't much rate Evans, but he felt sorry for him nevertheless. He knew what it felt like to be the centre of unwelcome attention, the scapegoat-in-waiting.

Bowman cleared his throat. 'Let me summarise,' he said, sweeping the room with his hawk's eyes. 'The situation, as I understand it, is this. We no longer know where Ms Rogers is. She left work early without being observed by us. She is not at her father's flat and she is not at her own. In short, none of you has any idea where she might be.'

Bowman paused. No one commented, though Reid saw five heads nod. Bowman's assessment was harsh, but you could hardly quibble with its accuracy.

Bowman turned his gaze towards Ashcroft. 'Sergeant, I presume we are not able to trace her mobile?'

'Correct,' Ashcroft replied.

Sergeant! Reid tried to show no sign of minding. The game of divide and conquer had started.

'Any credit or debit card activity, Sergeant?'

'Not so far, sir.'

'And what about the bomb, Sergeant? What can you tell me about that?'

'Standard home-made incendiary device,' Ashcroft said. 'Detonated remotely, probably via a mobile phone.'

'But no one killed or injured.'

'That's correct, sir.' Yes, sir, no, sir, three bags full, sir. Ashcroft was brown-nosing for all he was worth.

'How many people were in the shop when it went off?'

'None, sir. We were lucky. No customers at that moment and no staff either. Ms Rogers was just across the road and Mrs Gupta had run out in pursuit of a girl who had stolen an apple.'

'I see.' Bowman spoke as if all this was new to him.

Reid had heard enough. He pulled a white handkerchief out of his pocket, shook it open and blew his nose noisily into it. Everyone looked at him, which was, of course, his intention. 'I'm not sure "lucky" is the right word.' He spoke to the room at large. He hoped he sounded casual. 'I would personally use the word "deliberate" to cover what happened.' He returned the handkerchief to his pocket and looked around. He was gratified to see that he had everyone's attention. 'Assuming the person holding the mobile was in the vicinity, with a view of the shop, my guess is that he or she wasn't interested in killing people, merely in damaging the shop.'

Bowman blew his cheeks out. 'Are you saying that the attack on the shop has nothing to do with Ms Rogers?'

It had become a conversation between the two of them. The rest were mere onlookers.

'I didn't say that, sir.' Reid wasn't going to go down without a fight. 'I suspect the attack on the shop has everything to do with Ms Rogers. But it must also have something to do with the girl. She came into the shop, she provoked a scene in front of Mrs Gupta and then she ran off with an apple. Mrs Gupta ran out after her and then someone detonated the bomb.'

Bowman's fingers were steepled in front of his face. 'Are you suggesting that the small girl's role was to draw Mrs Gupta out of the shop?'

'I think that's possible.'

Bowman nodded, slowly and rather theatrically. 'It seems complicated,' he said eventually. 'If all you want to do is destroy the shop, why not just blow it up after it's shut? Why not pour petrol through the letter box in the middle of the night and throw a match in?'

Reid leant back in his chair. He could have pointed out that the shop had a metal grill which ensured that no one could poor petrol through its letter box at night, but he doubted that such an observation would be well received by Bowman. He responded with another question. 'Why did the girl and the man who was with her come to the shop? There must have been a reason. Someone or something must have drawn them there. Presumably it was something to do with Ms Rogers. Anyway, if we knew the answer to that, then the chances are we'd also know the motivation behind the bombing.'

Reid fell silent. The carriage clock on Bowman's desk whirred into life.

'And what about the smoke bombs?' This time Bowman was looking at Reid when he asked the question.

'Different from the firebomb, sir. Manual timers set to go off simultaneously. Designed to cause confusion rather than damage.'

'I understand the thinking behind smoke bombs, Inspector,' Bowman said tartly. 'But what was the point of them yesterday?'

Reid tried not to react, though he could feel the muscles down the right side of his face doing a Jumping Jack Flash impression. 'Ms Rogers is the common theme as you know, sir. She was working in the Italian café next to the bookshop that was targeted. She appears to have been very helpful getting people out of the premises. Very cool in the circumstances. Too cool perhaps.'

'Too cool? What the hell do you mean by that? Do you have some reason for saying that? Like evidence?' Bowman had half risen to his feet. His face was flushed. Reid realised with a start that Bowman was on the verge of losing his rag. That was something he had never seen before.

Reid shrugged. 'I merely meant that Ms Rogers didn't seem exactly surprised by the turn of events. It was almost as if she was expecting it.'

'You mean she may have been responsible for the smoke bombs herself?'

'I didn't say that, sir.'

Bowman opened his mouth, but whatever he was about to say remained unsaid. Instead he loosened his tie and released the top button of his shirt. This, Reid knew, was not a good sign.

'What about the CCTV coverage? Can anyone enlighten me on that? His eyes flicked around the room and settled, as before, on Ashcroft.

'That was interfered with, sir. In the bookshop the cable had been cut and in the newsagent someone had poured superglue into the recording mechanism.'

Bowman was still standing, rocking on his feet from left to right.

'What about the other CCTV cameras in the street? They can't all have been malfunctioning. I want to know what Ms Rogers did yesterday from the time she turned up for work until the time she left. Now get out of here, all of you.'

They stood up as one, anxious to escape.

'Not you, Evans,' Bowman snarled. 'I want a word with you.'

* * *

Maggie stood over the bed and looked down at Beth. The girl had finally and definitely fallen asleep, curled up on her side in a foetal position. With her number one haircut she could have been a boy, but the defiantly pink nightie gave the lie to that. Her breathing was effortless and even. In profile her nose was slightly up-turned and her chin jutted forcefully out. Maggie shivered with grief and long-buried memories. The girl looked so like her mother it was scary. And like her mother, she would turn heads throughout her life. Maggie had no doubts about that.

'I miss my mum.' That had been the last thing Beth had said before collapsing into sweet oblivion.

'I miss your mum too,' Maggie had replied. 'She was my best friend ever.'

'So where have you been all these years?' That was what Beth could have said. But she didn't. Maggie was grateful for that.

'Sweet dreams,' she whispered and retreated from the oasis of Beth's room and shut the door behind her with a click. She remembered her own mother saying that to her. She had liked it.

Sam was on the edge of his bed, rocking backwards and forwards again.

'Sam,' she said, trying to getting his attention.

He continued rocking. His eyes were fixed on the wall.

'Talk to me,' she said, her voice rising sharply in tone and volume.

No response.

'For crying out loud, Sam, talk to me.'

Sam slowed, very gradually. Eventually he stopped rocking altogether. Now he sat, rigid except for the slightest shake, head cocked as if he was listening to something far away.

'I lied,' he said. He turned to look at her, as if to gauge her response.

'About what?'

'About Ellie.'

'What the hell do you mean?' She said this in an urgent whisper, fighting the urge to shout at him, conscious there was only a single door between them and Beth.

'It wasn't a hit-and-run.' There was a long pause. Sam was stock still, but panting fast as if he had just run up a steep hill. Maggie held her thoughts and her tongue, waiting for him to continue.

'It was six weeks and one day ago. She went out about six o'clock after the three of us had had a Welsh rarebit supper. I thought she was going to the gym. I even put Beth to bed.' He spoke haltingly, a sentence at a time, complete with full stops and pauses.

'Then she rang. She was really strange. Started to tell me how she loved me and Beth. She told me that I had to tell Beth that as soon as she woke up in the morning. Because she wouldn't be there to tell her herself.'

There was another long pause.

'What the hell are you saying, Sam? That Ellie walked out on the both of you? On her daughter? That's crazy. Ridiculous!'

Finally Sam looked at her and Maggie saw the agony in his face. 'She shot herself, Maggie. Right there, on the phone. She said goodbye and . . .' He waved his hands in the air in despair. 'Bang!' He clapped his hands against his temples, again and again, harder and harder. 'Bang!' Then he began to cry.

* * *

'Why would Ellie kill herself?' Maggie said. Five minutes had passed since Sam had dropped the bomb of

62

Ellie's suicide into the room and he's said nothing since. He had sat on the bed, intermittently rocking backwards and forwards as if in time to music only he could hear.

'Tell me, Sam,' Maggie said. 'Was she depressed? Had something happened?'

'I don't think so,' he said.

Outside in the corridor a man and a woman stumbled past. He was talking urgently and she was laughing.

Maggie waited until she heard the door slam shut behind them.

'Christ, Sam, you must have noticed!' She hissed the words, leaning forward towards him, conscious of the child in the adjoining room.

He stood up and walked over to the window. He pulled aside a corner of the curtain and peered out. Then he turned round. '*They* did it,' he said.

Maggie felt like grabbing him and shaking the truth out of him. But she didn't. She straightened herself. 'Who are *they*?'

He shrugged. 'They wanted Ellie dead, and now they want you and me dead too.'

Maggie tried not to jump to conclusions, but it was hard not to, given what she knew about Sam. Coming out of Sam's mouth *they* could mean anything: his own paranoia, the voices in his head, the man who he had imagined was watching him on the bus, the woman at the supermarket till, the news presenter on the TV.

'Sam,' she said sharply, forcing him to look at her. 'Why did you come to the shop?'

He closed his eyes and swayed like a poplar in the wind. 'I couldn't leave Beth, could I? Not for a moment. Not with them out there watching. But I needed to find you. I thought she would be safer dressed up. That way, no one would recognise her. She loves being Snow White. She really got into it. What with picking through the apples and accusing the woman of poisoning one.' Sam's torrent of words stopped. He smiled. It was the smile of a proud father.

But Maggie had no intention of letting it rest there. 'Was it you who set off the firebomb in the shop?' It was an accusation, not a question. The only thing that was missing was the word 'why.'

Finally Sam opened his eyes. He rubbed the sockets with the palms of his hands. The image of the three monkeys popped into Maggie's head. Hear no evil. See no evil. Speak no evil.

'Of course I didn't. What the hell do you take me for?'

'So it was just a coincidence that you came to the shop that evening and that as soon as you left there was an explosion. Is that what you're telling me?'

'Of course it bloody well wasn't!' He lurched up from the bed, so that he stood towering over her, swaying. 'If I knew all the answers, I'd tell you.' He was angry. The vein down the left-hand side of his face was pulsing in a way she remembered. She flinched in anticipation. Not that she had ever known Sam to be someone who would hit a woman. But she had pushed him hard and everyone, she imagined, had their breaking point. Yet all that happened was that he walked over to the bathroom and shut the door carefully behind him. She heard him talking to himself, his voice rising and falling like a wild sea. It had been so long that she'd almost forgotten that this was how he was.

'Is Sam OK?' Another voice, but behind her. Small and anxious. Maggie turned. Beth was standing in her doorway.

It was always 'Sam,' never 'Dad.'

* * *

Evans arrived at the rendezvous ten minutes early, feeling like he had won the lottery. Not the jackpot, but a prize nevertheless. When Bowman had told him to stay behind, he had expected the worst. But Bowman's bark had turned out to be worse than his bite.

'This is your chance to make up for your stupid mistake, Evans,' he had said as he handed over a small jiffy bag.

'Deliver this tonight. Don't ask any questions. And come straight home when you've done it. I want you on duty with Reid and Ashcroft in the morning. Without fail.'

So here he was, two hours' drive away, parked in the road just outside the Jubilee Hotel, waiting for his contact to arrive.

'Stay in the car. Don't use the car park. She will come to you.'

Evans didn't know her name. He didn't know what she looked like. 'Best if you know nothing,' Bowman had said.

Evans watched. A couple were advancing towards him along the pavement, but they walked straight past. A young man in a bomber jacket, hands thrust deep into his pockets, followed.

Then someone tapped on the window. Evans jumped in alarm.

A woman peered in at him. She had a cigarette in her hand. She gestured at him. Evans let the window down.

'Got a light?'

'I don't smoke.'

'Not my lucky night.'

Evans picked up the jiffy bag from the passenger seat and passed it to her. 'It is now.'

She took it and flicked the cigarette into the darkness.

'Go home,' she said.

Evans turned the car round and headed back towards the main road. He glanced in his mirror. The woman was still standing where he had left her.

CHAPTER SIX

Maggie woke to the comforting sound of water gurgling in the pipes. She lay on her back, eyes half open, soaking up the peace and wondering what time it was. There was no sound of Sam — snoring or breathing or talking — and no sense of his beanpole body in the room. Before she had gone to bed, she had wondered if he would try it on with her, and she had been a bit miffed when he hadn't, not because she had wanted either him or even the temporary solace of sex, but because it would have been nice to have been asked. She wasn't sure how she would have reacted if he had.

She heaved herself up and swung her legs over the side of the bed. That was when she saw that Beth was standing in the doorway, fully dressed in football kit. 'When are we having breakfast?'

Maggie looked around. There was no sign of Sam at all.

'He's gone out,' Beth said, reading her thoughts. 'I'm hungry.'

Maggie showered as quickly as she could. Fifteen minutes later they were downstairs, in a huge restaurant with breakfast laid out on side tables and hotplates. Help yourself, the food said. So she did, to muesli plus some dried apricots and a dollop of yoghurt on top. She noted that Beth followed suit, but with a smaller helping. They sat together in a corner by the window, from where she could survey the whole room. There was no sign of Sam. She was tempted to ask the spotty young man who brought her a cafetière if he had noticed a very tall man eating earlier, but she decided against it. She told herself it was best not to draw attention to herself and Beth. Or rather, Matt. It was important to think of the girl as a boy or else sooner or later she would call her the wrong name and then someone would definitely remember them.

'Well, Matt,' she practised, 'how about some bacon and egg?'

A pair of blue eyes regarded her warily. 'That would be very nice,' the child said, adding after a pause, 'Mother.'

They sat eating their hot food in amiable silence, except when the child looked across and said, 'This is delicious, Mother.'

'Glad you are enjoying it, Matt,' she replied, playing along.

Maggie watched the girl-boy with fascination. How did mothers behave towards their children at breakfast in a posh hotel? Because this hotel was definitely posh, if a bit worn, like a film star in her twilight years. And she wondered, not for the first time, how it was that Sam, the impoverished activist, was familiar with it.

'Such a shame Father didn't wait for us,' the child said. 'Don't you think, Mother?'

Maggie held a finger to her lips. Beth was overdoing it now, sounding like a character from some black-and-white film. Mother and Father indeed! Did the upper classes even talk like that anymore? She doubted it, just as she doubted that Beth had ever called Ellie, 'Mother.' More likely it had been 'Mum' or possibly 'Ellie.'

After breakfast Beth insisted on using the lift, even though it would have been quicker to take the stairs to the first floor. As they were waiting for it to come, Maggie felt a small hand slip into hers. She didn't dare look down, but she felt something primeval, a lurch of emotion so intense that she felt giddy. Inside the lift, their hands remained locked together. Only when they were back in the room did Beth release her hold, but even then they remained standing side by side for several seconds, unable to move, bound together by feelings that neither yet understood.

It was the child who broke the silence. 'Where *is* Father?' she said. Even in the privacy of their room, she was still playing a part. Or was she?

Maggie wanted to say something reassuring, but she couldn't because, like Beth, she had a feeling — a gut-wrenching fear in her case — that Sam had left them. It wouldn't be the first time he had walked out on her. Instead, all she could do was insist that the child brushed her teeth (wasn't that the sort of thing good mothers did?) before she would allow her to switch on the TV. Sticking your child in front of the TV was, she imagined, the first resort of a lazy mother. But Maggie needed Beth to remain safe and secure in the room while she went downstairs and nosed around. She wanted to know if Sam had really gone. If so, she would have to start making plans fast.

* * *

It would be asking too much for the platinum blonde with the heavy make-up and the cleavage to be on reception. If anyone at the hotel knew where Sam had gone, it would surely be her, but of course she was nowhere to be seen. The man standing in her place was young and — she soon realised — Polish.

'I'd like to pay for our room,' she said. 'Although we aren't quite ready to leave yet.'

'Of course, madam. Your room number, please?'

She told him and waited while he checked his computer screen.

'Ah!' He straightened up. 'The bill has been settled. I remember it. The tall gentleman paid for it, just as I was starting my shift."

'What time was this?' she asked.

'I start at seven o'clock.'

'He left the hotel after he had paid?'

The man shrugged. 'I think so. But I notice he had no luggage.'

'Did he take a taxi?' she asked. How else would he get away from here? She doubted any buses ran down these country lanes.

'He did not ask for one.'

She scratched the side of her head. What on earth was Sam playing at? Had he left for good? Why hadn't he told her? Perhaps she shouldn't have been surprised. People don't change. Not people like Sam, at any rate. Maggie looked at the receptionist, but he was doing something on the computer. Or pretending to. She sensed that he was avoiding her gaze.

'Pavel,' she said, having belatedly taken in the name badge on his jacket pocket, 'tell me, how did he leave the hotel? Did he just walk off?'

Pavel looked up from the vital computer activity he was engaged in. Again there was a refusal to look her in the eye. He seemed to be finding a spot above and beyond her left shoulder hugely fascinating. 'I think Sinead gave him lift,' he said eventually.

'And who is Sinead?' she asked, even though she was pretty darned sure she knew precisely who Sinead was.

'Sinead was on duty last night. She finished her shift at seven o'clock this morning.' Pavel's smile was nervous. Possibly he was afraid she might make a scene. Eventually he looked directly into her face. 'The gentleman wants to leave at seven o'clock. She finishes at seven o'clock. So she offers the gentleman a lift. That is kind of her, no?'

Kind, my arse! The words were on her lips and it took a huge effort to stop them from going any further. She told herself she needed to be forgettable. Which was all very well, but Sam's height made that difficult. And now Pavel was sure to remember her if anyone came asking.

'And is Sinead likely to be working the late shift tonight?' She tried to sound casual.

'I am not sure, madam.'

'Can you find out?'

'But, madam, you will not be here tonight.' Pavel wasn't as slow as he looked.

Maggie shrugged. 'No matter.' Anyway, she told herself firmly, even if she could get to speak to Sinead, what would Sinead be able to tell her? Sam would hardly have divulged his plans to her, would he?

The problem with doubts and suspicions is that once they slip into your consciousness, they become very hard to dislodge. As Maggie trudged up the stairs back to her room the questions inside her head swirled thick and fast. Who exactly was Sinead? Sam hadn't brought them to this hotel by chance. He had come for a specific reason, and that reason had to be Sinead. And now he and Sinead had disappeared and she had been left behind with Beth. Was that always Sam's plan, to palm his daughter off on her before doing a runner with Sinead to God only knew where? And was Beth his daughter anyway?

When Maggie got to the bedroom, she paused. It was time to put on her super confident, I'm-in-charge-and-I-know-what-I'm-doing face. 'It's only me, Beth,' she said as she pushed the door open.

Beth was sitting on the bed, engrossed in the TV. Beyond her, also on the bed and also watching was a woman with blonde hair and a magenta-and-white striped top. She turned towards Maggie and beamed at her.

* * *

70

Elgar stood outside the back door and admired the view. Not that it was an extensive one, but it was pleasant enough. In the foreground were grass fields populated by sheep safely grazing. Beyond the sheep were dense fairy-tale woods which separated them from whatever it was that lay beyond. There were deer in the woods. He had seen three of them on a previous stay. But he had seen none that morning, not even when he had scanned the edge of the woods with his binoculars soon after dawn. Maybe, if nothing happened, he would take a walk later and see if he had more luck.

He was smoking his first and only cigarette of the day. He did this slowly and methodically, admiring the lengthening ash in between puffs and reflecting on the power of nicotine. He had once been a thirty-a-day man and he took pride in the fact that he could now smoke one a day and not relapse. It was a matter of self-control, and a test he set for himself every single day. Self-control was essential in this job. The day he smoked a second cigarette would be the day he needed to jack it all in.

The door opened behind him. He didn't have to turn to see which one of them it was. He had worked with Bridget long enough to be able to distinguish her tread, and her cloying perfume was something of a giveaway.

'He's having breakfast,' she said. She had a glass of water in her left hand and a gun, complete with silencer, in her right. Elgar made no comment. She was always prepared. The chances of Arthur making a run from this place were as remote as the Hindu Kush. The doors and windows of the safe house were fastened tight. The only way out for the old man would be via this back door.

'No news then?' Elgar knew it was a daft question to ask her, but sometimes daft questions were better than none.

'Something will happen.' Bridget sipped at her water, calmness personified. 'It always does. Sooner or later.'

'Those two aren't your average idiots, you know,' he said. He had studied their background. He didn't believe in underestimating people.

'You remember what they say, Elgar?' She gave him one of her inscrutable smiles. Elgar said nothing. He knew that another Chinese proverb was poised on the tip of her tongue. 'When you are dealing with an idiot, that's when you most need your wits about you.'

She wasn't calling them idiots, of course. Elgar knew that. Her words were aimed at him. She might as well have been pointing her gun right between his eyes. Idiot! She was goading him again. Elgar shrugged. He wasn't going to get dragged into her games. He knew she was trying to get him to react. The question was, why.

'Your turn to babysit the old man,' she said. She tipped the rest of the water onto the ground and handed him the glass. 'I fancy a walk.'

Elgar said nothing. He watched her saunter down the path and out of the picket gate. He was puzzled. What the hell was she playing at? *I fancy a walk*. Bridget Malone never fancied a walk. She wanted to get away from him. She wanted to speak to Bowman where she couldn't be overheard by Elgar. She was trying to cut him out of the loop. Suddenly Elgar was certain of that. But he still didn't know why.

* * *

'Hi, there,' the blonde said. 'Nice to meet you again, Maggie. By the way, my name is Sinead.'

'What exactly are you doing in my room?'

'Been having a nice chat with Matt.'

'I'd like you to leave.'

'Or rather Beth.'

Maggie felt a chill run through her.

'I'll ask you again. What the hell are you doing in my room?'

72

Sinead gave her a lopsided smile. 'Don't worry, honey. Sam brought me up to date with everything. Matt or Beth — doesn't matter to me. Sam and I are old friends, if you know what I mean.'

'Old friends?' If she had wanted to rub Maggie up the wrong way, she could hardly have chosen two more effective words. 'Where the hell is Sam anyway?'

Sinead shrugged. 'Dunno. Honest.' She showed no sign of getting off the bed. She stretched out her perfectly shaped legs. She was wearing brown leather boots over jeans. She flicked an invisible speck off her thigh. Maggie felt a surge of jealousy.

'You gave him a lift somewhere,' Maggie said. 'Pavel told me.'

'Into town. He said he had things to do.'

'What things?' Maggie snapped. She could feel her self-control unravelling.

Sinead flipped herself up off the bed like some show-off gymnast and slipped on a black leather jacket which was lying over the back of the one armchair in the room. 'You know what Sam is like. He never tells you more than the minimum.' Sinead moved round the bed and up to Maggie. 'But he asked me to give you this.' She held out an envelope.

Maggie snatched it without a word of thanks. She was furious: with Sam for playing silly buggers, with Sinead for her hour-glass figure, cool manner and gorgeous perfume, and with herself for being so ridiculously jealous of the woman. She ripped open the envelope, glanced at the sheet of paper inside it and stuffed it into her back pocket. She had known what it would be — another of Sam's rows of numbers, another coded rendezvous. 'Did he say *anything*?' she snapped.

Sinead ran her hands through her mane of hair. 'Gotta go.' She zipped up her jacket until it tightened over her breasts. Her face tightened too, suddenly serious. 'Out the back way. You never know who might be watching.'

* * *

'So remind me, what exactly is it we're looking for?'

There were three of them inside the lift's tiny cubicle — Reid, Ashcroft and Evans. The doors had shut, but as yet there was no sign of upward movement. Already Reid was feeling the first tell-tale signs: dry mouth, sweat on his forehead and a heart that beat crazily fast. But the last thing he was ever going to do was admit to claustrophobia in front of the ambitious Ashcroft and the incompetent Evans.

'You'll know when you've found it,' Reid replied as the lift juddered into life.

Several seconds later — and not a moment too soon for Reid — they were emerging into a corridor with pale green walls and mottled, darker carpets. And very shortly after that they were inside Maggie Rogers's apartment. 'I'll take the living room,' Reid said. It was, fractionally, larger than the bedroom, which was dominated by a double bed and a large, freestanding wardrobe.

What *were* they looking for? The truth was Reid had no idea. Searching the flat was one of the things that had to be done, but if Maggie Rogers was as smart an operator as she appeared to be, it was unlikely she would have left anything incriminating or helpful lying around.

Twenty minutes later, the three of them were standing together in the living room.

'Well, what now?' Ashcroft said in a disgruntled tone of voice.

Reid shot his sergeant a filthy look. They had drawn a blank and Ashcroft's insubordinate manner had resurfaced like a persistent U-boat.

'Back to the office,' he said, and he pushed his way out of the flat, leaving Ashcroft and then Evans to trail behind. Which was why neither Reid nor Ashcroft saw what Evans did next.

What he did was pat himself just above the heart, checking that the contents of his inside jacket pocket had not somehow dematerialised since he had slipped them in less than three minutes previously. Then he followed his two senior colleagues out and shut the outer flat door firmly behind him.

* * *

Beth sat in the back of the car while Maggie drove. She always sat in the left-hand back seat. 'It's safer in the back,' her mum had told her, and she liked to sit on the left because that way she could see the driver.

She had buckled herself in and was inspecting the contents of her rucksack. She only had three sets of clothes in it, and one of those was the football kit which Sam had given her. She hoped she wouldn't have to wear it again. She had three DVDs (*Frozen*, *Bambi* and *Sleeping Beauty*), a hairbrush and comb, toothbrush and toothpaste, a nightie, slippers and her little jewellery box with a tiny ballerina painted on the lid. She opened it. Inside was a necklace which her mum had given her, two friendship bands that she had made at a festival they had gone to, and now also a bracelet which the woman in the hotel had given her. Maggie didn't seem to like the woman. She didn't know why, because the woman had been very nice to her. She had told Beth how she and Sam had known each other for years. Anyway, the bracelet had little red jewels studded around it. 'Costume jewellery,' the woman had called it. 'My mother gave it to me, but it is too small now and I don't have a little girl to give it to, so why don't you have it.'

Beth had been thrilled. It was so pretty. She had put it on her wrist and then held it up to the light.

'Sam might not approve. Probably best not to tell him. Or Maggie.'

Beth shut the box. Tonight, maybe, she would put it on in her bedroom. She would wear it while she was asleep.

She looked up guiltily, in case Maggie had noticed, but she was still studying her road atlas. 'Is everything all right?' Beth asked, but Maggie just grunted.

'Haven't you got a GPS?' she asked. Mum had had a GPS. The woman on it had spoken in a rather strange voice. 'I could change it,' Mum had said more than once, 'but the last thing I want is to be told how to drive by a man.' She had laughed every time she said it. Beth wished it was Mum in the front seat now, not Mother Maggie. Mother Maggie was nice, but Beth missed Mum's jokes.

'No, dear, I haven't.' Mother Maggie was peering out through the windscreen as she answered. The rain had appeared from nowhere, drumming hard on the car roof and the windows were steaming up fast. Beth hoped she would be able to see where she was going. She put her hands together and shut her eyes. She would pray for a safe journey. Mum had insisted that she say her prayers every night. And every night she had prayed that God would keep Mum and her safe, and Sam too, though sometimes she didn't bother to include Sam because half the time Sam wasn't there.

The prayers hadn't worked in Mum's case though. One night she had gone off and never come back. Even so, praying for safety seemed better than not praying for safety. So she did.

She must have fallen asleep, because the next thing she knew the car was bumping to a stop. Maggie pushed open the front door. 'Here we are,' she said.

Beth got out too. It had stopped raining. The sun was trying to break through the low cloud. And there, standing under a tree was a familiar figure: Sam. She gave a squeal of delight and ran to hug him.

'Hi, Beth. You been looking after Maggs?'

'What on earth have you been doing?' Maggie snapped. 'And don't call me Maggs. I hate it.'

Beth released Sam. She didn't want them to argue. Her mum and Sam used to argue. She wanted Maggie to be nice all the time.

He held up the plastic bag he was holding. 'Getting some insurance.' He grinned. 'A set of registration plates in case we need to throw them off the scent.'

Beth wasn't sure what he was talking about, but at least Maggie shrugged and stopped telling him off. 'You'd better put them in the boot.'

* * *

'Do you have any idea what the hell is going on?' Maggie said this to Sam as soon as Beth was safely inside the shop. She didn't know how long it would take the girl to buy herself some sweets. She had given her three pounds, and as soon as she saw Beth running eagerly across the garage forecourt she had felt a stab of guilt. Three pounds for sweets? That was surely the act of a bad mother. Three pounds worth of flavoured sugar and fat. Not that Beth was in danger of putting on weight. But Maggie knew all too well how bad food habits could lead to obesity and how difficult it was to reverse the process. A pound would have been plenty.

Sam didn't answer her question immediately. He was staring off into space. Maggie wasn't sure he had even heard what she had said. But just before she opened her mouth to repeat herself, he turned and looked at her. 'They're fishing.'

If Sam was trying to wind Maggie up, this was the perfect answer — a real steam-out-the-ears one. She clasped her hands together and counted silently to three. 'Why did you come to the shop, Sam, and why did you bring Beth?'

'Matt,' he said.

Maggie swore. 'It's not a game, Sam, for crying out loud.'

'They offered me a deal.'

'A deal?'

'They said they would protect Beth if I did what they wanted.'

Maggie swore again. 'And you believed them?'

'What alternative was there?'

This time Maggie didn't reply. They both sat silent in the car. Sam turned on the CD player. Bob Dylan kicked into immediate life, droning on about how times they were a-changin'. Sam had always liked Dylan, but he had only ever been a passing phase for Maggie, a musical fling. He had seemed to promise the world for people like Ellie and herself, but it had all been a mirage. She and Sam had argued viciously about him once. At least, she had been vicious. 'A protest poet who struck lucky. A sexist bastard.' Or words to that effect. Anyway, as far as she was concerned it didn't feel like the times had changed at all.

Maggie bit back the urge to resurrect that distant spat. 'For God's sake, Sam, don't go silent on me.'

He was still moving his head in time to the music.

'Sam!' It was a final warning.

Sam's head slowed imperceptibly until it was just a tremor. 'I thought I could keep one step ahead of them,' he said.

Maggie let out a screech of frustration. 'For crying out loud, Sam, you couldn't keep one step ahead of a one-legged octogenarian!' That was totally unfair, and she knew it. He was pretty clever at keeping ahead of things and people. But she needed him to engage with her and to acknowledge that they were in deep shit. 'They tried to kill us, all three of us. You, me and Beth!'

Sam turned reluctantly towards her. 'No they didn't,' he said.

'What are you talking about? They blew up the shop.'

'No they didn't,' he parroted. He was still looking at her, impassive, giving away nothing. Then he did something with his face, sucking in his cheeks and blowing out his nostrils. 'I blew the shop up,' he said quietly. 'Once I knew there was no one inside to get hurt.'

'You what?' For several seconds her brain went into freefall.

Sam gave one of his trademark shrugs. 'I wanted to confuse them.'

Maggie swore. Maggie lifted her hand and touched her face under the left eye, where she'd had a couple of stitches. 'You also did this, you moron. A piece of glass. One inch higher and I could have lost an eye.'

Sam's face twitched momentarily. 'But you didn't, did you?' He turned away, lost again in Bob Dylan. 'I guess that will have confused them all the more. They'll be wondering who the hell did plant the bomb.'

* * *

Beth wasn't sure that three pounds was going to buy her that many sweets, not after she had got a bar of milk chocolate for Sam and something for Maggie too. Because Maggie — or Mother as she really must try to think of her — was actually quite nice and she really would have to buy her something or it wouldn't be fair. Mum had always insisted on things being fair. She had no idea what Mother would like. Maybe mints or chewy fruits or maybe she was a chocolate person, like Sam. Anyway there was a chocolate bar on special offer for ninety-nine pence, so she got that, and after she had examined several bags priced at ninety-nine pence she settled on wine gums for Mother and jelly babies for herself. That all seemed very fair indeed. She put them in her basket and wandered back along the aisle. The man behind the counter was watching her. He smiled and called out, 'Found what you want, young man?'

She didn't reply. This was partly because she had forgotten that she was dressed to look like a boy and partly because something had caught her eye on the shelves in front of her. This was where the newspapers and magazines were laid out. And in the middle of the display were several comics. Not that she was that interested in them normally. But the one on which her eyes were fixed was no ordinary comic. She picked it up, stared at the cover for several seconds and then began to leaf through it.

'You like Disney, do you?' It was the man behind the counter again. 'There's more than one there.'

Beth acknowledged him with a brief smile and closed the comic. She looked at the rack again. The man was right. The Disney magazine behind the one she was holding had a different cover. She picked it up and then leafed through the ones behind it. She pulled out another. Three different ones! For several seconds she battled with herself before putting the second one back on the shelf. Two was enough, especially when they were so perfect. One had a feature on Bambi and the other had several pictures from Snow White and the Seven Dwarfs. She added them to her basket and advanced to the counter.

'Right-o, my friend, let's see what you've got.'

Beth watched him. She didn't have nearly enough cash, but she wasn't worried because she knew what she would do.

'I'll pay with this,' she said, waving a debit card at him.

He frowned. 'Is that yours?'

'My dad's,' she said. 'He's out there in that silver car with my mum. You can go and ask him if you want, but he's got mental health problems so he might not like it.' She smiled at him. Mum had always said she had the smile of an angel and already in her short life she had learned how effective it could be.

The man licked his lips and frowned. He looked out of the window across the forecourt. Then he turned back to her and shrugged.

'OK. So you know the pin code?'

'Of course not. But all I have to do is tap it. Right?'

'Right.' The man spoke slowly. He was, Beth reckoned, rather stupid. She had seen Sam tap his card in the corner shop at home and the coffee shop in the high street. He had even let her do it once or twice.

'Dad will get cross if I take much longer,' she lied. 'And so will my mother.' She gave another smile. 'They might think you're chatting me up.'

She wasn't sure what chatting up involved, but she had overheard Sam and her mum discussing it in relation to one of the teachers at school.

'OK,' the man said. 'You can tap your card now.'

* * *

Abingdon's market square was empty. That didn't surprise Evans. It was nearly six o'clock, but rain was lashing diagonally across the market square, and no one in their right mind would want to be out in that. Bowman was late. The prerogative of rank, Evans supposed. He pulled his mackintosh closer around him and tried not to care. At least the Corn Exchange offered protection from the rain, though he was half soaked already, just from walking from the car park.

At least I am in Bowman's good books, he thought to himself. At least he is making use of me. After the cock-up with the tailing of the Rogers woman, he had thought he was for the high jump, but that turned out not to be the case. Quite the opposite.

'Evans!'

He jumped and turned.

Bowman shook his umbrella and closed it. 'Not much bloody use in the wind.'

'No, sir.' Evans felt a spike of annoyance that the old man had managed to get so close without him noticing. The Corn Exchange was open on three sides and he thought he had got all the angles covered. How on earth had he failed to spot him?

'Sorry if I took you by surprise.' Bowman smiled as if he was joshing. But Bowman didn't do joshing. He was making a point. Even Evans recognised that.

'So, show me what you've got.'

He handed over two envelopes. Bowman adjusted his glasses on his nose and studied the envelopes. The writing was distinctive and arty. The lettering was almost but not quite joined up and the ink was reddish brown. Both were addressed to Maggie Rogers c/o Hairdelicious. Bowman grunted and opened the two envelopes, reading and then replacing the single sheets of writing without comment. Evans had read them himself, of course. They were short and circumspect, asking politely after Maggie, wishing her a happy birthday in one case, and telling her in both cases a little about how Beth was growing up.

Bowman slipped the envelopes into a pocket inside his coat and buttoned it up again.

'What do you make of them, Evans?'

Evans had anticipated the question, but even so he wasn't sure how to respond. 'They aren't exactly gushing,' he said. 'Just an attempt to keep in touch. Tell her how her daughter Beth was.'

Bowman grunted. 'Who runs Hairdelicious?'

'A woman called Zoe Fisher,' Evans replied. He had anticipated that question too. 'I've got her home address.'

'Ah, of course. Zoe Fisher.'

'You know her, sir?'

Bowman didn't answer. He merely nodded in a way that suggested that this all made sense to him. 'I think we should pay Zoe Fisher a visit.'

Evans felt pleased that he had done something right. He wasn't sure that Bowman liked him or rated him very highly. But then Bowman didn't seem to like anyone. Praise from his lips was rarer than hen's teeth.

'Right,' Bowman said. 'We'll take my car.'

* * *

Zoe Fisher lived three storeys up in a block of unexciting flats overlooking the Oxford ring road. Evans must have driven past them often enough, but he had never noticed them before. He suspected they were fairly recent additions to Oxford's housing stock.

'I'll do the talking,' Bowman said just before he pressed the bell. Evans nodded. He was relieved. The last thing he wanted to do was make a pig's ear in front of Bowman. Better to observe and learn how Bowman the Bastard handled a hairdresser.

The door opened almost immediately. Evans was surprised. It was as if she had been expecting them. The woman was, he guessed, in her forties, with tinted orange-brown hair, pursed lips and a face tinged with bitterness.

'Oh!' she said. Her disappointment was obvious.

'Police,' Bowman said abruptly and he held up his ID in front of her face. 'Are you Zoe Fisher?'

She studied the ID suspiciously.

'I'm sorry to bother you at this time of night, but we really do need to talk to you.'

'I'm expecting company,' she said.

'It won't take long.' Bowman pushed his way in past her.

'Oi!' she said. 'I didn't say you could come in.'

Evans was impressed by her spirit. He could never in his wildest dreams imagine saying 'Oi!' to Bowman.

'Tell me about these.' Bowman held up the two envelopes, one in each hand like a card trick.

'Look, what's this all about?' Fisher put her hands on her hips.

'It's about you answering some questions. When you've answered them — and only when you've answered them — my colleague and I will depart.'

Fisher would have been only a fraction taller than Bowman in her bare feet, but her precipitous high heels gave her a considerable height advantage. She looked down on him and he stared up at her and for a few moments there was stalemate. Then she crumbled. She waved her hands in a gesture of defeat.

'What is there to tell? They were delivered to my salon.'

'When?'

'I dunno. Haven't they got postmarks with dates?'

'When?' he snapped, holding them up in front of her face. 'Roughly speaking?'

Fisher opened her mouth to say something, then closed it.

Bowman waited. He didn't say anything. His face was half-hidden in shadows cast by the several candles which Zoe Fisher had recently lit. He exuded menace. Evans could feel it. He almost shivered.

Zoe Fisher shrugged and gave way. 'I guess one came about a year ago, maybe. And the other maybe a year before that.'

Even though Fisher's hands remained firmly attached to her hips, Evans could sense that she was nervous. He wondered why.

Bowman continued his questions. 'You know who they are from?'

'How should I? I don't read other people's letters.'

'Not even the one that came the other day?'

For a moment Zoe Fisher was taken by surprise. Evans saw her mouth open and then close like a fish suddenly pulled from the water. She licked her lips nervously. Eventually she said, 'Of course not.'

'You gave it to Maggie then?'

'Yeah, I did. When she came in for her trim the other day.'

'What did she say about it?' Bowman seemed to have an unlimited arsenal of questions, each primed and ready to fire.

Fisher's hands came away from her hips. She dragged her fingers through her hair. Evans began to feel sorry for her.

Fisher pulled out one of the chairs tucked beneath the small dining table and sat down on it. She looked up at Bowman's shadowy face. 'What Maggie said was, "Thanks." Like any normal person would. Then she put it in her bag. And that was it.'

'So you had rung her and warned her that another letter had arrived?'

'No, I hadn't.' Fisher's defiance was still there, if struggling. 'She was booked in for a haircut. Why would I have rung her? It was just a letter.'

Bowman put the envelopes back in his jacket pocket and buttoned up his coat.

'And you weren't just a tiny bit curious about who these mysterious letters were from? And why they were being sent care of your hairdressing parlour? I would have been if I were you.'

'Maybe, but I didn't ask.'

'Are you and Maggie friends, then?'

'No,' she replied.

Bowman snorted. It was something he often did. Evans called it his pig impression. 'Thank you,' Bowman said. 'Sorry to have bothered you. We'll be off now.'

Evans followed Bowman down the three flights of stairs. When they were outside he summoned up the courage to ask him how he knew there had been another more recent letter.

'It was a guess, Evans,' he said, easing himself into his car. Evans opened the passenger door and got in.

Bowman started the almost noiseless engine. 'Evans, I want you to get a check done on Zoe Fisher's phone for the last year. I want to know if she's had any contact with Maggie Rogers apart from the booking of her haircuts.'

'First thing tomorrow, sir.'

'No. Now, Evans. I want the results by first thing tomorrow. And remember you are reporting to me on this, not to DI Reid. Now off you go.'

Evans paused uncertainly.

'Out!' Bowman gestured with his left hand. 'I've got to get home or the wife will kill me. You can make your own way back to your car, can't you? The buses are still running.'

Evans levered himself out of the car and shut the door carefully behind him. He would like to have slammed it, but his instinct for self-preservation was too strong. At least he knew the area. It would take him over five minutes to walk to the bus stop. Then he'd have to go right into the centre before catching another bus out to Abingdon. It would take at least an hour.

'Of course, sir. I'll catch a bus, sir,' he said to no one as Bowman drove smoothly off up the road. He waved sardonically into the darkness and watched as Bowman's rear lights grew smaller and smaller. Bowman turned left, which was exactly the route Evans was going to have to walk to get to the bus stop.

'Bastard!' he shouted into the empty street.

* * *

When DI Reid heard the knock on his office door, he groaned audibly. It was late and he wanted to get home and he knew without even looking up that the dot-dot-dash-dash belonged to Ashcroft. He hadn't forgotten Ashcroft's weaselly performance in front of Bowman and he certainly hadn't forgiven it either. One day he would teach him a lesson.

'Sorry, boss.' Ashcroft's face appeared warily from behind the door.

Reid glared at him. His sergeant was rocking nervously from foot to foot.

'I just thought you'd want to know about this straight away.'

Reid said nothing. He took a sip from his coffee, keeping his eyes on his sergeant.

'He's used his debit card.'

'He?'

'Sorry, sir. Samuel Foulkes, sir.'

Reid smiled inside. Ashcroft's penitence was rather pathetic, yet very satisfying. He motioned him to sit down. There was no need to rub things in at this stage. He would bide his time. 'How about some details, Sergeant?' he said.

'Sixteen twenty-five hours this afternoon. In a garage just south of Gainsborough.'

'Gainsborough?'

'North-west Lincolnshire, sir.'

'How much fuel did he buy?'

'None, sir. He only spent nine quid. We reckon it must have been food.'

'And why the hell wasn't I told this before now?'

Ashcroft flushed at the sudden savagery. 'It only came through to us ten minutes ago, sir.'

'Well, it bloody well shouldn't have. It's critical information. And all it tells us is where he was several hours ago. He could be anywhere by now.'

Ashcroft nodded. 'I agree, sir. I told Evans to prioritise it. But I guess if Foulkes has used it once, the chances are he'll use it again. Probably today.'

Reid considered this. Maybe Ashcroft was right.

'Also, sir, it has occurred to me that if Foulkes was planning on driving a lot further, wouldn't he have put some fuel in the car? In which case, maybe the Gainsborough area is where they were headed. Maybe they are holing up somewhere round there.'

This made sense and yet Reid wasn't entirely convinced. From what he had read in the files on both Sam Foulkes and Maggie Rogers, they were both pretty smart operators and using a bank card to buy food or whatever didn't seem that clever.

'Well, sir?' Ashcroft had sunk back into his chair, relaxing a fraction.

'Go through everything we've got on them. Anything and everything. Why are they in North Lincolnshire for God's sake? Is it someone they know? Did one of them used to go on holiday there? Or work there? Or have a granny or a lover who lived there? We need to find them. Fast.'

* * *

'This is nice.' Beth looked round the bedroom, taking in the floral bedding and curtains, the pink wicker chair and the dressing table with a mirror all the way along the back of it. She sat on the stool in front of it and stared at herself. She saw Sam's reflection. He was watching her in that way he had when he cocked his head to the side. As if there was something he was puzzled about.

'Can we stay here for more than one night?' she said as she unzipped the rucksack and began to lay its contents out on the dressing-table surface. Her Snow White costume and wig, the doll, her DVDs, loom bands, a necklace which she had made with her mother at a holiday art class and her new magazines.

She glanced up at Sam, but still he didn't answer her question.

She looked back at herself in the mirror, at the short hair and the football shirt. 'I've had enough of this kit,' she said. 'I don't want to be a boy any more. I want to be me. Or Snow White.'

Sam remained silent.

She got up and carried the magazines over to the bedside table. She wanted to read them later.

'Beth.'

'What?' She didn't look at him. If he was going to ignore all her questions, why shouldn't she ignore him?

'We believe in telling the truth, don't we?' he said.

She felt uneasy. That was the sort of thing that her mum used to say, usually after she had received a letter from school. That was the tone of voice she used too, all calm and lovey-dovey.

'Let me see those magazines.'

'Why?'

'Please.'

She shrugged. Right at this moment she was really missing her mum. 'I didn't think you liked Disney.'

He held out his hand. She had no choice. She picked them up again and handed them over.

He looked at the covers.

'You got them today, in the garage shop?'

She nodded.

'You didn't steal them?'

'No!' She wasn't sure why he was making such a big deal about it. It had always been Mum who fussed about this sort of thing. Her mum. She felt tears welling up inside her. Any minute now, she would start crying and that was the last thing she wanted to do, especially in front of Sam.

'So you paid by cash?'

Beth walked back to the stool and sat down on it.

'What does it matter?'

'Where did you get that much money from?'

'I used your debit card,' she said.

'What?'

'I found your bank card in the hotel. On the floor. So I thought I'd look after it for you. You don't mind, do you?'

But Sam clearly did mind. She could tell because he used a rude word that Mum used to get very cross about. His face turned serious. 'Give me the card, Beth.'

She unzipped one of the side pockets of her rucksack and handed it over.

'Next time, use cash,' he said. And he gave her a five pound note in exchange. 'Alright?'

'Alright,' she said.

* * *

Maggie was singing softly to herself. It was seven in the evening. Sam had suddenly announced that he had to go and meet Sinead and he had left. Beth had begged Maggie if she could 'please, please, please!' watch her

89

DVD of Frozen and had been engrossed in it for the last twenty minutes. So Maggie had retreated gratefully from the fray, first to the loo and then to the small but wonderfully appointed kitchen to make cocoa for the both of them.

It was such a relief to have a few moments to herself. As she sang Nora Jones's "Come away with me," she felt the stresses of the day begin to recede. Stirring the milk on the hob was a simple, peaceful act. Through the doorway, the happy sounds of *Frozen* were suddenly muted, though it took several seconds for Maggie to register the fact. When she turned, she saw Beth standing in the doorway dressed in her Snow White outfit. She looked small and lost.

'I really miss Mummy,' she said.

Caught off guard, Maggie nodded. She lifted the saucepan off the hob and poured the steaming milk into two mugs, stirring as she did so. It felt like an important moment. What on earth do you say to a child who says she misses her dead mother? She felt totally unprepared.

She placed the mugs on the small pine table in the centre of the kitchen. 'Let's drink here,' she said, 'so we don't spill the cocoa. Then we'll watch the rest of the film together.'

Beth sat down dutifully and pulled her mug towards her, wrapping her delicate fingers round it. She sniffed. 'Was it wrong to use Sam's bank card?'

'Of course not.'

'It's not stealing, is it?'

'No.'

'Sam was cross. When he's cross, he goes really quiet.'

'Don't worry,' she said, before changing the subject. 'Why don't you tell me about Mummy?'

Beth screwed up her face as she considered this. 'She always read to me at bedtime. Even if she was going out, she read to me. I would read to her a bit too, but she was really good at it. She could make a person sound angry or sad, mean or kind. And she was brilliant at animals.'

Maggie sipped at her own cocoa and saw the child mimic her movements. She felt like a fraud. Who was she to sit here and probe this poor child about her mother when she, Maggie, had fallen out so spectacularly with Ellie? She thought back to the hotel, and the moment when Beth had slipped her hand into hers while they were waiting for the lift. She thought about the ridiculous pleasure she had taken from hearing the child call her 'mother,' even though it was an act. Mother indeed!

'*The Gruffalo*,' Beth said, cutting into Maggie's reverie. 'That was the last story we read. It was my favourite, though I'm getting a bit old for it now. Mum liked it too. She sat on my bed and we took turns to read the words and make lots of silly noises. Then she looked at her watch, gave me a kiss and said, "Got to go. See you in the morning, love." But she didn't, did she?'

Beth sipped at her cocoa and Maggie wondered if she should say something comforting or just wait for the child to continue.

'I waved at her out of the window . . .' Beth paused. Little wrinkles creased her forehead. 'But Mummy didn't see me. She just got into a car and went.'

A car? Maggie was suddenly on full alert. Sam hadn't mentioned any car. 'What sort of car was it?' If Sam wouldn't talk to her, then Maggie would have to quiz Beth, as long as she did it tactfully.

'It was a lovely big black car, but the windows were all dark so once Mum got in I couldn't see her. I wanted her to wave back at me through the window. Perhaps she did and I just couldn't see her.'

Beth pushed her mug towards the centre of the table. 'I'm tired,' she said. 'Do you mind if we watch *Frozen* another time?' Her tone was far too old and sensible for her years.

Upstairs she brushed her teeth and got into bed without a murmur. 'Can you say a prayer for me? Like Mummy.'

And so Maggie, who had never in living memory said anything approaching a prayer, made something up. Then she sat by the bed until the girl's breathing settled into the unmistakable rhythm of sleep.

* * *

The rendezvous was typical of Sam. It took place in a filling station that had been razed to the ground. Sinead arrived fifteen minutes early. He was twenty minutes late. She wasn't in the slightest bit surprised. Same old, same old.

'Any problems getting here?' he said, as if it was he who had been kept waiting.

'No.'

He stepped closer and put his arms around her. For several seconds they stood there like that. She hugged him back, surprised all over again at how good it felt to have his body pressed against hers, how strong her feelings for him were, in spite of everything.

'So it went well this morning?'

'Sure.'

'You gave Beth the bracelet?'

'Yes.'

She felt his arms tighten around her, more like a vice than a hug now. 'Sam!' she squeaked. Anxiety flared within her. Had she misjudged him? What was he playing at? 'Sam!' Her voice rose. 'You're hurting me.'

He grunted and released her. He stepped backwards. 'I knew I could rely on you.'

'Now we are quits. You did me a favour and I did you one. I have my own life to live.'

'Not so simple as that, sweetie.' His right hand went to her jacket. She flinched. He slid the zipper up until it reached her neck. She knew he was using her. Buttering her up so she would do something else for him. She had been on the receiving end of his techniques enough times in the past.

'So what do you want me to do?' she said, brushing his hand away and stepping back a pace. She had had enough of his games. She wanted to cut to the chase and get it over and done with — whatever 'it' was.

Sam pulled a wallet out of the back pocket of his jeans. The sky was clear and the moon was full enough to show her that it was fat with cash, but what he gave her was a debit card and a piece of paper with a four-digit number.

'Drive north until you get to Penrith. Go to a cashpoint and withdraw three hundred pounds from it. Then chuck the card away. Make sure you park at a distance from the cashpoint because the chances are there will be CCTV. Make sure you can't be recognised. Wear the anorak I'll give you. Drive home by a different route. Forget you ever knew me.'

'That seems simple enough. And I guess you're going to head off in another direction?'

Sam didn't reply. He didn't do words when silence would suffice. She followed him to the car. He extracted the promised anorak from the boot and handed it to her. He leaned forward and gave her a quick squeeze. 'Thanks, honey. Now, go!'

* * *

More than two hours had elapsed since the detectives' visit, but Zoe Fisher was still on the most dangerous of edges. So when the doorbell rang, she almost squealed. She stood stock still and waited. The bell rang again, more insistently this time. Her anxiety levels were bouncing around like helium-filled balloons in a wind tunnel. Perhaps the police had come back. They had found out that she had not told the whole truth — God only knew how they had found out — and they had come back to grill her again, maybe even take her down to the police station. She padded softly along the carpet and not for the first time cursed herself for not having had a spyhole installed in the flat door. Carefully she slipped the security chain into position. She took a deep breath and turned the catch, allowing the door to open just ten centimetres. She peered through the gap and saw a face she didn't recognise. Red hair, bright wide-open eyes and a distinctly expensive perfume.

'I'm a friend of Maggie's. Alice King. I've got a message for you. She doesn't want to ring you or come here in person because she's worried that she is being tracked. Can I come in?'

Zoe slipped off the chain and let her in.

'What the hell is going on?' Zoe gasped before bursting into hysterical tears.

It took several minutes for Alice to calm Zoe down. She tried talking to her quietly, but that had no effect. She found a half-drunk bottle of white wine in the fridge and gave her a drink, but if anything that made things even worse. Finally, she removed Zoe's glasses from her nose and gave her a single sharp slap. That worked.

'Do you want to talk about it?' Alice said. 'It might help.'

So Zoe talked — about the police, about Maggie Rogers and about the letters. Alice was the perfect listener, occasionally asking a question, but mostly just keeping quiet and paying attention. Zoe wondered if Alice had had professional training. Maybe she worked for the Samaritans in her spare time.

When Zoe finally fell silent, Alice said, 'Would you like a neck massage?'

'Oh God, yes!' Zoe replied. 'A neck massage and then an early night is just what I need.'

Zoe sat up straighter and allowed her eyes to close. Sometimes she had clients who fell asleep while they were having a haircut. That was what she hoped would happen to her while Alice massaged. A lovely dreamless sleep.

And that was what did happen, in a way. Zoe felt something soft and gentle drift around her neck, but it was gentle only for a second or two. Then it tightened viciously, so that she coughed and choked. 'Alice!' she gasped, as she tried desperately to claw herself free from the scarf, now tight around her neck. But in less than a minute she was unconscious and shortly after that she was dead.

'Not Alice,' the woman said as Zoe sank into oblivion. 'Bridget.'

Bridget searched the flat methodically but with limited success. There were no more letters. No diary. No nothing, except for Zoe Fisher's mobile. Amongst all the photos were two selfies of Zoe and Maggie in a bar somewhere in Oxford, taken three months previously. Not exactly world-shattering, but it did show that Zoe had been lying about the friendship. More fool her.

* * *

Sinead reached Penrith just after 9.30 p.m. If Sam had been with her, he would have insisted on driving around until they located an out-of-the-way parade of shops. But in her book it was a lot easier just to head for the large supermarket in the centre of town. She pulled up on the far side of the car-parking area where one of the overhead lights had failed. She swapped her leather jacket for the anorak, pulled up the hood and wrapped a scarf around her face. Then she made her way to the bank of cash machines, put in the card, entered the PIN that Sam has given her and withdrew £300. Simple. There was only a scattering of parked cars. A young couple in a battered Ford Focus nearly bumped into her as they exited the supermarket in a hurry. They were stuffing what looked like Krispy Kreme donuts into their faces.

Sinead walked unhurriedly back to her car, removed the anorak and put on her leather jacket, scanning the area again as she did so. Nothing and nobody to worry about. Inside the car, she studied the bank card for several seconds before tucking it into the zip pocket above her left breast. Then she started the engine and headed out of town and onto the motorway heading south. She drove for nearly an hour before pulling up at some services. After a visit to the toilets, she bought herself a black Americano and returned to her car where she stood, sipping it. Her right hand played some half-remembered tune on the zipper of her jacket, up down, up down. She barely noticed the chill northern breeze which was blowing a crisp packet across the tarmac. The coffee was strong but too bitter, and eventually she tossed the cardboard cup, still half full, into the nearest bin. She extricated her mobile from an inside pocket and flicked through the contacts list until she found the number she had been looking for.

She should have checked in earlier, at Penrith at the latest. Really she should have rung through after her meet-up with Sam. But Sam and she went back a long way. She spat the last of the bitter taste of the coffee into the darkness. She flipped the phone shut and stuck it back in her top pocket. To hell with Bowman. He could wait until morning.

* * *

Back in the kitchen, Maggie had located a bottle of Chilean Merlot. She poured herself a generous glassful and opened up her tablet. The house belonged to one of Sam's friends, or so he had said. Maggie was doubtful, but Sam had known where to find a spare set of keys (hidden under a flowerpot no less) and she hadn't been in a mood to question him. The heating worked, the cooker worked and so too (she assumed) would the Wi-Fi. She entered the password — conveniently written on a small square of ivory card pinned to the kitchen noticeboard — and waited.

Her brain was spinning. Sam had never mentioned Ellie getting into a car. Hadn't he known? Did he not ask her where she was going that night? Did she regularly get into big black cars of an evening? When Sam had originally told her that Ellie had been killed in a hit-and-run, Maggie had imagined Ellie walking off up the road to the gym or maybe going on a run after dark. Carelessly cutting across the road as the rain came down, straight across the path of a car driven by a man with a mobile phone attached this ear. Bang! Then Sam had told her that Ellie had rung him up and blown her brains out while he was listening. Bang.

Maggie pushed these thoughts to the back of her brain. The internet had finally sparked into life on the tablet. She started to search. It shouldn't be that difficult to find details, she told herself. She knew where Ellie had lived. She knew the date — or near as dammit. Suicides got reported. A woman obliterating herself with a bullet through the head was news, especially for the local press. Post-mortems were carried out. Funerals were held. Bad news was always good news as far as the media is concerned.

'. . . I just can't believe it, she was such a nice woman.'

'Loved her daughter. Always ready to help.'

'You would never have guessed she was so unhappy.'

Maggie could have written the newspaper reports for them. All that crap. So trite, but often true.

Almost immediately Maggie came up with several hits for Ellie Nelson. Mostly they were from several years ago, when she had appeared in court for taking part in demonstrations at the local airbase and a controversial bypass project. In one photo, she was standing next to a woman who had shrouded her face with a long scarf. She didn't need to peer at that one to know who Ellie's companion was. She could recognise herself even though the Maggie of those days carried a lot less weight than she did now. She moved on. There was a grainy photo of Ellie chained to a tree and a tall guy in a balaclava half turned away, anxious to preserve his anonymity. Sam probably. She stared at the screen, peering closer. Definitely Sam. Other articles revealed how Ellie had been fined on one occasion and given a short suspended custodial sentence on another. There was a more recent and less controversial moment — a photograph of her and Beth standing with various other mums, dads and children outside a family centre which had just been saved from the austerity guillotine.

But however much Maggie searched, no matter what words she searched on, she could find absolutely no report of Ellie's death.

* * *

It was as if the door and the mobile were connected. Sinead slammed the former behind her and immediately the latter began to ring. It was past midnight. It could be one of only two people — Sam ringing to check she had done what he had asked, or . . .

Two initials, 'BB,' flashed blue on the screen. She stared at the phone, lying in the palm of her hand. An unexploded bomb. She wanted to ignore it, but she knew that would only make things worse. She placed it on the table, accepted the call and switched on the loud speaker.

'Hello, sir!' she said as perkily as she could manage.

'What the hell have you been playing at?'

'Just got in, sir.'

'You are meant to report in.'

'Sir.'

'Regularly.'

She could feel her heart hammering. 'I was about to ring.'

A pause. She tried breathing slowly, in . . . out.

'Liar!'

The word seemed to reverberate around the flat. Sinead stood with each hand pressed flat against the table, her head lowered towards the mobile. How much did he know?

'Why in God's name did you go to Penrith tonight?'

For a moment Sinead thought she was going to be sick. She fought the sensation and tried to think. It must be her mobile. They had been tracking it. Of course they bloody well had! And if Bowman didn't know by now that someone had been using Sam's debit card in Penrith tonight, he soon would. And then he would put two and two together and make four.

'It was Samuel Foulkes,' she said, trying to pretend to herself that this was a simple debriefing over the phone. 'He asked me to drive to Penrith and use a debit card there to withdraw some cash from an ATM. Then I was to throw the card away and return home.'

'And did you throw it away?'

'No.'

'Good.'

There was another pause. Sinead waited. Her heart was still palpitating crazily.

'Sinead,' he said, 'Did Foulkes say anything else? Does he want you to meet up with him?'

'No. He told me to go home. I had served my purpose.' That was Sam all over. Use you and then discard you — until he needed you again.

'So where was he going while you were busy leading us on a wild goose chase to Penrith?'

'He didn't say.'

'You must have some idea.' Bowman's voice had gone dangerously quiet.

'Sam doesn't give information away.' Sinead began to speak quickly. She knew she probably sounded flustered to Bowman, as if she was not sure what story to tell him, but she had no way to control it. 'You know what he's like,' she continued. 'He tells me the minimum. They were holed up for the night but he didn't say where. Then they were moving on somewhere which was obviously not Penrith.'

Bowman gave a grunt. There was more prolonged silence, during which Sinead could hear his laboured breathing. Eventually he said, 'How is that little boy of yours?'

She shivered. Bowman didn't do polite conversation, at least not with her. Probably not even with his wife.

'He's with my mother tonight.'

'That's nice.' Another pause. Had Bowman once been on a course called *A beginner's guide to the use of the pregnant pause to scare the shit out of people?* He would have passed with flying colours. 'Tell you what, Sinead, I suggest you line up your mother to keep him for another night or two.'

CHAPTER SEVEN

It was not yet five, but Maggie was wide awake. She stumbled to the loo, splashed some water over her face and returned to the bedroom. She turned on her sidelight and dressed quickly in the clothes she had taken off only four hours earlier.

'Sam?' She leaned over him and gently shook his shoulder, but all he did was twitch and give a slight snort.

She nodded, satisfied. Sam might think he was clever, with his cryptic codes and devious ruses, but when it came down to simple cunning, she was a match for him.

She had sat up waiting for him, watching some third-rate Liam Neeson film on TV, until he appeared at about half past eleven. She had left the wine bottle on the kitchen table and he had, predictably, downed a glass within a couple of minutes of collapsing next to her on the sofa. She had gone to the kitchen and brought the bottle through, filling his glass again and emptying the remainder into her own. Liam Neeson had just killed a couple of thugs when Sam put his glass — again empty — on the table and laid his hand on her thigh. Her leg jerked violently as if she had just spotted a tarantula on it. Her glass, still full, catapulted across the room and smashed against the stone surround where the wood burner sat.

'What the hell are you playing at?' she had snarled.

'Hey!' He held up his hands in a gesture of mock surrender. She had seen it before. Turning it into a joke. Making out it wasn't an issue. As if wanting a quick grope was nothing. Just a bit of inebriated fun.

She got up and started to pick up the pieces of glass in silence.

'Jesus, Maggs. You know how I feel about you. Just for old times' sake, hey?'

'Not even for old times' sake!' she snapped.

He swore and stood up. 'Off to bed.' And he stumped off up the stairs.

She remained on her knees, searching for shards until she heard his heavy tread along the corridor above her and into the double bedroom.

By the time she had got upstairs, he was lying on his back on the double bed, snoring softly. Which was pretty much what he was doing now, at just gone five in the morning. He looked as if he hadn't shifted position all night. Not that Maggie was surprised. Two large glasses of wine was more than she had planned on him drinking when she had added the sleeping drugs to the bottle. Well, he should sleep for several hours yet, by which time she would be miles away.

And Beth would be miles away too, because there was no way she was going to leave the girl with him. Maggie didn't trust him further than she could spit. He had lied about Ellie. Why, she didn't know, but Beth was safer with her, and if she owed Ellie anything it was to keep her daughter safe. She would be a mother to her in whatever way she could.

So by five fifteen, a drowsy Beth was strapped into the back of the car, their bags were in the boot, and they were on their way. Maggie felt confident that she had stolen a march on Sam as well as whomever it was he was working for. It would be hours before he woke up and even longer before he would be able to raise help. She had taken his mobile — turned off so that they couldn't be tracked — and tucked it away in her handbag, along with all the cash she had found in his wallet. She had smashed his tablet PC with a large stone from the garden rockery. She had done the same to the Wi-Fi router in the house. She had removed his shoes to slow him down if he decided to run off to a neighbour's. And finally, she had left a trap for him, a *coup de grace*. A small part of her was ashamed that she had stooped so low, but it was tiny. The longer it took for Sam to raise the alarm, the more chance she had of doing what she knew she had to do. Because now she was convinced that Sam was part of the plot.

* * *

Sinead received the text at six thirty-five. She awoke instantly, even though she had had barely five hours' sleep. Over the last few days, sleep had become somewhat elusive, to say the least.

The text was from Bowman. No courtesies. Not even a verb. Just a time and a place.

She sat up and tried to think. Now what did he want of her? Hadn't she done her part? She had done exactly as he had instructed — or nearly. Sinead just wanted her life back.

She went into the bathroom and showered, washing her hair twice and soaping her body until the water ran cold. Then she went into the galley kitchen, made some fresh coffee and poured herself a bowl of muesli.

She knew she had to go along with it until she had paid her debts to the bastard. What choice did she have?

Her mobile beeped again. It was her mother. 'Jake just woken up. Slept like a log, bless him! Do you want to come over for lunch?'

Jake was the love of her life and her weakest point, as Bowman knew. 'How is that little boy of yours?' he'd said, and it hadn't been from concern. It had been a warning, a reminder that he held the power. There was a chain which bound the two of them together and she knew deep down that Bowman would never let his end go.

So what the hell was she going to do? Go along with him meekly, or . . . or what?

She was still working on an answer when her mobile began to ring. It was a number she didn't recognise. Should she answer? She had no real choice. She answered it.

* * *

Bowman was sitting on the balcony of his top floor flat admiring the view. He was wearing a coat against the early morning chill. His mobile rang. Sinead, he thought, ringing to wheedle or argue. But it was that arch-creep, Ashcroft, sidestepping Reid. Bowman allowed himself a glimmer of a smile. Nothing like a bit of dissension in the ranks.

'Yes, Ashcroft?' He spoke calmly. 'I trust this is important. I don't generally like being rung by sergeants at this time of the morning.' Or any other time either, he might have added. Sergeants reported to inspectors.

'I believe this is important, sir. I haven't actually informed DI Reid yet. He's asleep at his desk. But I thought you might like to know as a matter of urgency.'

'Know what?'

'They're in Penrith.'

Bowman's brain whirred even faster than usual, but he said nothing. Keep the man hanging. If Ashcroft was waiting for a pat on the back, he wasn't going to get it.

'Can you hear me, sir?' Ashcroft said.

'How do you know, Sergeant?'

'They've used Foulkes's bank card in Penrith. Took three hundred quid from an ATM in the early hours.'

'I see.' Bowman weighed his options. One was to simply relent and say something appreciative. So he did just that. 'Good work, Sergeant.' Toss a sprat to catch a mackerel. It had been one of his mother's favourite expressions. 'It looks like they are heading for Scotland, then.'

'That's what I reckon, sir.'

'Good thinking.' Massage the man's ego, he thought. Pat him on the back and send him in the wrong direction. 'Well, Sergeant, don't let me delay your search. You had better tell DI Reid now. But keep me informed,' he said and rang off.

Bowman remained at the table, tapping his fingers. His coffee was cold, and he had no time to make a new one.

He stood up and leaned against the railing of the balcony. Down below, men and women were heading off to work. A bus was pulling away from the stop immediately below him. A man with a black refuse bag in one hand was rooting around in a bin, looking for breakfast. Bowman saw all this, but it didn't register.

He smiled to himself. It was all coming together rather well. Ashcroft and Reid would now head off towards Penrith on their wild goose chase and would be well out of the way while Bridget and Elgar tied up all the loose ends. Because if they didn't soon, the loose ends were in danger of unravelling.

He flicked through the contacts on his mobile until he found the one he was looking for. Then he made the call.

A mocking, Irish voice. 'Good morning, William.' Only Bridget ever called him William. Except for his wife, of course. To everyone else he was either 'Bill' or 'sir.'

Not that he cared too much. Bridget was the only person he could trust implicitly. The one person he needed.

'I've got an extra little job for you, sweetie.'

'Oh, William! You are going to wear me out with all these extra jobs.'

'Her name is Sinead.'

* * *

'Aaagh, shit!' Sam had woken from his drug-induced sleep with the thickest of thick heads. When he peeled his eyes open, he had absolutely no idea where he was. He lay there trying to remember the night before, without success. When that didn't work, he pushed himself up on his elbows to look around. Immediately a big bass drum exploded into action in the back of his head. He shut his eyes and held himself still, hoping that the pain would disappear. It didn't. He opened his eyes again and squinted around the room.

There was a three-quarters full glass of water on the far bedside table. Maggie's, presumably. She must have slept there, next to him. She must be downstairs having breakfast, or maybe it was long after breakfast. He groaned and swore simultaneously.

The fog was beginning to disperse. Slowly. They had to get going. He swung his legs over the edge of the bed and padded to the bathroom. There were painkillers in the bathroom cupboard. He took two, and then a third, washing them down with tap water.

Beth's was the only other room upstairs and the bed was a mess. But there was no sign of her bag.

He went back onto the landing and listened. Not a sound. He called their names, but quickly decided that they weren't going to answer. He switched on the light in the main bedroom and felt anxiety for the first time. Maggie's small red case, the sort you take as carry-on luggage on a flight, was nowhere to be seen.

He turned and stumbled as quickly as he dared down the steep panelled staircase. 'Beth! Maggie!'

Then . . . 'Aagh! Shit!' His feet exploded in agony and he crashed to the floor, narrowly missing the kitchen table. For several seconds he lay still, fighting the excruciating pain and the impulse to yell like a baby. As he pushed himself up off the floor, something sharp pierced his right hand. He swore again.

Glass! He could see three pieces embedded in the palm of his hand. And there were lots more, he knew, embedded deep in both his feet. He lay there for several seconds, dazed and trying to work out his options.

Eventually he levered himself up onto a chair and tried to inspect the damage to his feet. He shifted himself onto the table so he could get a better view outside. He swore again. The car had gone. Maggie, Beth and the car were all gone.

* * *

'They're moving, sir.'

It was 7.30 a.m. Reid had had five fitful hours of sleep in his desk chair and he felt crap. He was pretty sure that Ashcroft hadn't even knocked and now he was standing in the open doorway with a Cheshire-cat grin smeared across his face.

'Late last night they used the card outside a supermarket in Penrith,' Ashcroft was saying. 'Took three hundred cash from an ATM. They must be heading for Scotland.'

'Why Scotland?' Reid was thinking aloud, but Ashcroft answered.

'Foulkes is half Scottish, sir.'

Reid looked at Ashcroft, giving him the full benefit of his dislike. 'And the other half is English.'

Ashcroft's grin stiffened. 'He heads north and stops at Penrith. Supermarket and garage are both open all night. They stock up on cash for fuel and food. You don't need to be a rocket scientist to work out that they are headed for Scotland. Where the heck else would they be going?'

Reid sniffed. He rubbed his chin. Ashcroft was probably right. It was the obvious conclusion. They were running short of cash, so they had withdrawn the maximum amount possible in a single transaction and by now they could be anywhere in Scotland. But Reid certainly had no intention of congratulating his sergeant.

And something bothered him about it. It was the fact that Ashcroft's conclusion was the obvious one.

'Have we spotted their car? Got them on ANPR?'

Ashcroft's faint grin faded. It was the weak point of his case.

'No, sir. But . . .' Ashcroft dribbled to a halt, primarily because Reid had got up from his chair, turned away and walked over to the single window in his box of an office. He stretched his arms, trying to ease his various aches. He was getting too old for this. He stared out across the busy thoroughfare at the hideous 1970s concrete construction that was his view.

He turned round and snarled at Ashcroft. 'They aren't stupid, Sergeant. I'm sure I have already made that clear. They are perfectly capable of changing registration plates, changing vehicles, changing identities even. They know how to cover their tracks. So what you need to do is get hold of the CCTV footage from that garage and supermarket in Penrith and see if we can identify them and their vehicle. Only then will we have some chance of tracking them reliably.'

'But we keep monitoring the card?'

'Of course you do. But we don't put all our eggs in one basket, do we, Sergeant?'

'No, sir.'

'Not unless you want them scrambled all over your face, Sergeant.'

Ashcroft nodded and left, closing the door carefully behind him.

Reid leaned with his back against the window and sighed. He had overdone the eggs a bit, he thought.

* * *

It was all very well to drug Sam and get the hell away from him before he woke up. But Maggie knew you can't just run away. You have to run *to* somewhere — or someone. She had struggled with that conundrum half the

108

previous evening. Where on earth were she and Beth going to escape to? Leaving the UK was no option — the kid had no passport. Sam had tried to send their pursuers on a wild goose chase to Scotland. Or that was what she assumed. But was that a smokescreen, a device to get her running in the opposite direction? Was Sam on their side or hers?

Then, halfway through her glass of Merlot, the answer had suddenly jumped fully-formed into her head. Going through her shoulder bag, she had come across Ellie's latest letter. She had picked it up and looked at it again. She had examined the back of the envelope with its printed, 'I love Trident' slogan and the cryptic pencilled message: 'Maybe I should retire soon?'

Only suddenly it wasn't cryptic at all.

It had been a hot June day. A Saturday. They had been sitting on a rock admiring the view. It was one heck of a view, though Ellie's attention hadn't been fixed entirely on the cold dark water below or the peaks rising in the distance. Rather her eyes had been following a group of maybe a dozen rugged young men scrambling up the escarpment away to their left. She had even borrowed Maggie's binoculars to get a better look.

'You never told me about this!' Ellie had giggled. 'I think I shall retire here.'

Maggie had laughed. 'Behave yourself, Ellie. It's a bit late for all that.' And she had leaned over and patted her friend's stomach. Beth, four months after her conception.

'No, I mean it, Maggs,' she had said, suddenly serious. 'This would be the perfect place to retire. To get away from the world.'

Now that this memory had risen from Maggie's unconscious, it refused to budge. Whichever way she looked at it, she came to the same conclusion. Ellie's envelope was telling her where she was, or might be going. Quite why and exactly where, was a different matter. On that occasion they had stayed in a cottage above the village, one familiar to her from several childhood holidays. It had been owned by a friend of her father, though when she and Ellie had gone there the friend had been long dead and the cottage had become a commercial let.

So maybe that was where she needed to go now. If so, she had to work out how to get to North Yorkshire without being followed. If Sam was on their side, then they would know what car she was driving. It would only be a matter of time before the cameras picked her up on the road.

Beth was fast asleep, which was a blessing. So Maggie made her way back onto the M5 and then headed south at a steady sixty-five miles an hour, fine-tuning the plan in her head. Then, just as Beth was waking, she pulled off into a motorway service area complete with CCTV cameras and Automatic Number Plate Recognition system. The two of them made their way to the loo and grabbed a takeaway breakfast before putting fuel in the car and continuing their journey southwards.

At the next junction, Maggie pulled off the motorway and found a discreet gateway to stop in. There she proceeded to remove the registration plates and replace them with the pair which Sam had stashed in the boot. She knew it was a risk. If Sam was on the side of the bastards who were after her, then they could be looking out for these number plates too. But it ought to buy her a bit of time. Quite how much, she didn't know. But for the time being it was the best she could come up with.

Maggie turned the car round and rejoined the M5. This time she headed north, back the way she had come.

* * *

When your child's father rings up and begs you for help, it ought to be a no-brainer. You help.

Sinead had received the phone call from Sam seconds after the text from Bowman. Bowman had made what appeared to be a veiled threat. It wasn't the first time and she knew it was unlikely to be the last. Unless . . .

As for Sam, Sinead had never told him he was Jake's father. In her darker moments — driving back from Penrith for example — she told herself it was just as well. And would it have changed anything if she had?

Way back, she had been a port in a storm for him. It had lasted only a few days and then he had gone. Nine months later, she had given birth to Jake. She had said nothing then or since. On the rare occasions that Sam had stopped by — usually for a meal and a place to crash for the night — he had shown no interest in Jake's parentage. So she had never told him. What would have been the point?

Now, when he rang, Sam had sounded desperate. Maybe he was exaggerating — he knew how to press all the right buttons. Maggie had apparently gone off with the car, Beth and his mobile phone and left a pile of broken glass on the floor for him to stamp on. His right foot was a total mess. Fortunately, Sam was a man who always had at least one spare pay-as-you-go mobile in his possession and Maggie had failed to find it, stuffed under the mattress on his side of the bed. Whatever else she thought of Sam — and he occupied too much of her thoughts — he was resourceful.

'Don't use your own car,' he had said. 'They'll be watching out for it.'

So she drove the half mile to her mother's and asked her to keep her grandson for another day. 'And do you mind if I borrow your car? I've got a long trip to make and yours is so much more comfortable.'

Her rendezvous with Bowman was set for nine o'clock, giving her some sort of head start. Bowman would go ballistic when he realised she wasn't going to turn up, but she would take that chance. Once she had sorted Sam out, she would ring Bowman and make her apologies.

* * *

111

For the second time that morning, Reid looked up irritably from his desk to see his sergeant barging into his office without so much as an 'excuse me, guv!' Once more the flimsy door banged against the filing cabinet behind it. The partition wall shuddered.

'You've got to see this!' Ashcroft insisted, towering over the desk. He was looking more disreputable with every passing hour. Three buttons of his crumpled white shirt were undone, revealing unappetising glimpses of a hairy stomach. A coffee stain trailed down the right-hand panel. It reminded Reid of snail slime.

'The CCTV, guv,' he explained, oblivious to the effect he was having on his boss.

Reid had been on the verge of giving Ashcroft a bollocking, but he got no further than opening his mouth. The reality was that he was absolutely knackered and pretty disillusioned too. He was barely up to a game of tiddly winks, let alone a shouting match with his two-timing sergeant.

Ashcroft took his silence for approval and returned whence he had come. Reid got to his feet and followed his sergeant across the open plan space to a desk where an excessively eager geek called Harry was sat in front of a computer screen twice the size of his own. Harry had only been there a few days, but already he seemed to be the go-to guy for anything technical or boring. Sifting through CCTV was both.

'I reckon this is your target, sir. Pulling into the supermarket car park right here. The car goes left and out of sight here, but . . .' Harry did something clever and they were watching another camera. 'Three seconds later, here's the car again. Moving further left, until it gets out of visual range.'

Harry did something else clever. 'Map of the car park. I've marked in fuchsia the path the car took. It must have parked in the shaded green area, because otherwise it would be visible in some of the other CCTV. The red cross shows the site of the ATM where the withdrawal took place.'

Smarty-pants Harry paused. Upping the drama? Reid was feeling vinegar-sour. Harry flicked to yet another camera. 'This is two-and-a-half minutes later. A person in an anorak, hood and scarf over the face goes to the ATM and withdraws the money. An exact match, timewise. Then returns across the car park. Three minutes later drives out the car park.'

'Thank you.' Reid hoped his tone would pre-empt any further running commentary from Harry. 'So who is the registered owner of the car?'

'Sinead Parkinson.' Ashcroft jumped in before anyone else could steal his role as announcer of dramatic news.

'What do we know about her?'

'She's got some form. Bit of an agitator. Arrested twice for protesting and once for trespassing on MOD property. Two fines. One suspended sentence. After that she dropped off the radar. No more arrests or incidents in the last five years.'

'Any connection with Maggie Rogers?'

'Not sure. They could easily have met. But it'll be tricky to prove.'

'I'm not a court of law,' Reid snapped. 'I don't need proof. I need to know if there is any evidence that points strongly to them having a shared history. Have they ever lived in the same town or street? Cohabited? Shared a squat?'

'We can't rule it out,' Ashcroft said, on the defensive. 'Both protested in the 2006 anti-war march in London.'

'Half a million people went on that, for God's sake. So unless you're hiding a photo of them marching arm in arm down Park Lane, you had better try a bit harder.'

Nobody said anything. Someone wandering into the room at that moment would have felt the tension and backed straight out. Reid knew what a prick he was being but he wasn't going to admit it.

'What about her private life? Family? Lover? Kids?'

Ashcroft tried again. 'One child. Name of Jake. Started at the local primary school. No partner as far as we know, but we haven't had time to check that out. Her mother lives in the same town. Looks after the kid quite a lot while Sinead works at a hotel.'

'Right.' Reid had heard enough. 'Sergeant, you and me will go and pay a courtesy call on Ms Parkinson. Harry, you concentrate on her background. For now, I need addresses for her house, her mother's house and the hotel. And get an ANPR out for her car. Now let's get on with it.'

* * *

'What a mess!'

Sam was lying on the sofa, feet up on the arm rest, while Sinead examined his foot. She had tweezers, disinfectant and a roll of bandage next to her on the small round table.

'This may hurt a bit,' she said, and pulled a shard out of his heel.

He said nothing. He was trying to think, and not to show any pain.

She pulled at another piece of embedded glass and his foot twitched.

'Keep still!' she ordered. Her sympathy was buried deeper than the glass.

He studied her as best he could from his supine position. She was bent over in concentration, her blonde hair hanging untidily down. The roots were showing brown. Perhaps she sensed his gaze, because she gave an extra hard tug at a resistant fragment and snapped out a question — or was it an accusation?

'So what did you do to her to make her do a runner?'

Definitely an accusation. He didn't answer immediately. He was still feeling half-doped. Putting together a coherent train of thought was proving difficult.

He certainly wasn't going to admit to having attempted to grope Maggie. Not when the evidence of its consequences were so obvious.

'I don't think she trusts me.'

Sinead gave a snort. 'Are you surprised?'

He ignored the question. 'I mean, I reckon she thinks I'm the enemy. Playing a double game. Pretending to be her friend from way back when, but . . .' He paused.

'But what?'

'I feel I owe her.'

'Owe her what?' Sinead had stopped her ministrations and was looking directly at him, holding the tweezers as if they were a weapon. 'An old girlfriend, is she? Or a new one?'

Sam had been skiing just the once. On the fourth day, arrogant and bored with his teacher, he had skipped class and made his way up to the top on his own. After three days of bright sunshine it had turned cloudy, which was why he had mistaken a black run for a blue one. Suddenly he had been hurtling downhill very fast with zero hope of avoiding a very nasty crash. That was what it was like now. He tried an emergency stop.

'I need her.'

'You need her?'

He shut his eyes, half expecting her to dig her tweezers right into his foot — and keep on digging.

He tried to explain. 'I need her for Beth. I can't look after the kid on my own.'

He had thought that this would soften her up, win her over. An appeal on behalf of a motherless child. That should penetrate any woman's defences, surely? So he was amazed to see Sinead lurch to her feet. She picked up the roll of bandage and hurled it at his head. He caught it one-handed and was absurdly pleased with himself. Reflexes still intact then.

'You can finish it yourself!' She stormed from the room, through the kitchen and out, slamming the door behind her.

By the time he had finished bandaging his foot and jammed a shoe over it, she had returned to the kitchen and was making toast. Still smouldering, like the toast, she banged two plates on the table and some strawberry jam, then the toast.

'Eat!'

He did so obediently, calculating his next move. She thrust a mug of black tea at him, then sat on the far side of the table and busied herself with her own breakfast. Her anger was evident in every gesture, every time she wielded her knife, every time she brushed her hair from her eyes. When she glanced across at him, he thought he could see hatred in her eyes.

'Thanks for doing this,' he said. He was looking down at the crumbs on his plate, cradling his mug in his hands. 'I really owe you.'

It didn't break the silence, not immediately. But it didn't provoke a violent reaction either. He half expected her to throw something — a plate or a mug. That would be easier to deal with. She could let off steam, he would clear up the pieces and then she'd realise she'd gone over the top and things would settle down. He raised his eyes and saw she was studying him. Her eyes were red.

'So where do you want me to take you? Do you know where Maggie has gone?'

'No.'

More silence. Sam watched her push the last piece of her toast into her mouth. She chewed it slowly as if she was trying to work something out. He was happy with silence. He didn't want to talk or try to find out what was wrong with her. He was still trying to work out his next move.

He swallowed the last of his tea, stood up and put his dirty things in the sink. 'I need to make a call,' he said and opened the outside door.

'Who the hell to?'

He didn't answer. He shut the door quietly behind him, and hobbled down the rough driveway. Only when he was sure he couldn't be overheard did he make his call.

* * *

'It's me,' the voice said.

It was an unknown number as far as Bowman's mobile was concerned, but he recognised the voice immediately.

'What the hell is going on, Sam?'

'Maggie's done a runner.'

Bowman swore.

'It's OK. She's taken Beth with her.'

'I see.'

'She's got the bracelet, so you'll be able to track her.'

Bowman said nothing. He was trying to assess how this affected things. Mostly it was OK, except that Sam was stuck where he was and would need picking up.

'Sinead is helping me.'

'Sinead?'

'My foot is a mess. Maggie left a pile of broken glass at the bottom of the stairs and I walked straight into it. And since she's also taken the car, I rang Sinead and she's helping out.'

Helping out? Helping out Sam, but not keeping him, Bowman, in the loop! Fury gripped him. First Sinead had failed to report in the previous night and he had had to ring her. Now she had skipped their rendezvous and instead driven God knows how far to help Sam! And Sam had let Maggie and the girl do a runner. What the hell was their game? The plan had been for Sam to win Maggie's confidence and stick with her. Bowman liked to be in control, and he couldn't help feeling that things were

117

getting out of hand. He liked to keep his operatives separate too, reporting directly to him. Sinead and Sam were too damned close, that was for sure. But the bigger question was, what exactly were they up to? And then there was Maggie. Was she part of their game or were they playing her?

'There's one more thing,' Sam said. 'Maggie smashed my tablet.'

Bowman heard this, but said nothing. He was trying to assess this news and weigh up its implications.

'So what now, boss?' Sam said. 'I can't track her without a tablet.'

Boss? Sam never called him boss.

'I know that, you idiot.' Sam fell silent, waiting for a response. Bowman, let him wait, enjoying the moment. He knew exactly what he'd do now. Thanks to Maggie, he had got Sam where he wanted him.

'I'll text you a rendezvous point,' he replied. 'Just give me five minutes to check out where Maggie has got to.'

The bastard was playing him for a fool. He'd get him. And Sinead. *And* Maggie.

* * *

Elgar never overslept. Or so he liked to tell people when they asked. Of course, people rarely asked. On this particular morning, however, he didn't wake up until well after nine. When he checked his mobile for the time, his first thought was that it was wrong, but instinct and the brightness of the light through a crack in the curtains told him otherwise.

He swore, sat up and listened. All was silent upstairs. Downstairs a radio played some music. BBC Radio 2 he suspected.

He padded to the bathroom and stood in front of the mirror. He looked at a man well past his prime, almost old. Greasy hair now flecked with silver. Eyes dark, as though he hadn't slept. Dry, creased skin, tinged yellow. He touched the stubble on his chin and told himself (not for the first time) that he really ought to call it a day. Cash in his chips and retire to a little cottage near a river where he could indulge his love of fishing. Walk to the pub each evening for a couple of pints and to chew the fat. Maybe get himself into the darts team. He thought about all this and grimaced. The stuff of fantasy. It was more likely he would end up in a grotty bolt-hole on the edge of Birmingham with flyovers and car emissions for company.

Fifteen minutes later, he entered the kitchen area, shaved, showered and dressed. Two faces turned to look at him — one with an expression of unknowing blankness, the other with one of disdain.

'Not sure that it worked,' Bridget said.

'What?'

'The beauty sleep treatment.' She sniggered as if she was a schoolgirl just arrived from rural Ireland. But Elgar knew that she had grown up on the streets of Belfast and had the unrelenting viciousness to prove it.

He ignored her, said 'Good morning' to Arthur and switched on the kettle. Two slices of toast and a mug of strong tea later, he sat down at the table.

'Who are you?' The vacant face peered at him.

'I'm your carer,' he said. It wasn't entirely a lie. Elgar certainly felt more like a carer than a captor. As far as he could make out, Arthur had pretty much lost his short-term memory, but Elgar couldn't be absolutely sure. There were times when he wondered if the old man wasn't more on the ball than he appeared to be. Acting dumb and playing safe. Elgar understood that. Playing safe was embedded deep in his own psyche. Hence his current anxiety. His own name was an unusual and memorable one, not like John or Stephen. It was quite likely that when all Arthur's other memories of his capture had disappeared, the name Elgar might remain stuck in his brain, waiting to emerge when the police interviewed him.

119

If the police interviewed him. Elgar knew that as far as Bridget was concerned, Arthur was a loose end that would have to be tidied up when the operation was complete. He himself saw things differently. Arthur was a senile old man who could safely be left in some deserted lay-by to be rescued by a Good Samaritan. Killing him would be like killing his own father. He couldn't do it, even if Bridget could.

'I'd like to go to the toilet.'

'Over there.' Elgar pointed across the room and bit into his toast.

'Bowman rang,' Bridget said as soon as Arthur had gone.

'And?' Elgar sipped at his tea. He liked the combination of strong tea and sharp marmalade. It was a good way to start the day.

'Maggie's on the move.'

Elgar bit off another piece of toast and waited for her to continue. But she said nothing. He looked at her and wondered what it would be like to ram her face into a vat of marmalade, just to make a sticky point. He almost smiled. 'Where's she going? And what about Sam?'

'She's given Sam the old heave ho. Taken the car and the kid and headed south along the M5. Stopped for fuel at the services earlier on this morning, bought breakfast, headed south again. After that . . .' Bridget paused, savouring the moment, 'After that she and the kid disappeared from view.'

Elgar had been about to stuff toast into his mouth, but hand and toast stopped, hovering above the edge of the table. 'What do you mean?'

'Pretty straightforward, isn't it?' she sneered. 'No sign of the car on the cameras since she left the services. So she must have turned off the motorway and then either hidden the car or swapped cars or changed the plates. *Comprendez?*'

Elgar felt the anger rising inside. He tried not to show it. He gave what he hoped was a good-natured shrug. 'So she could be anywhere.'

'Not *anywhere*.' Another sneer. Another grudge for Elgar to harbour alongside all the others.

Elgar pushed the toast into his mouth and chewed. Suddenly the marmalade tasted like bile. He looked across at Bridget, doing his best to look bored.

'Are you going to explain what you mean exactly?' he said.

'We have a tracking device in the car.'

'*We?*'

'We, as in Bowman and us. Not as in Reid and the other plods who also report to Bowman.' She paused. Elgar waited. In the silence Arthur could be heard, straining and swearing. 'The girl is carrying a bracelet with a transmitter hidden in it. So we don't need ANPR to keep tabs on them. All we need is this.'

Bridget flipped open the tablet which was lying on the table in front of her and busied herself with it.

'So where exactly is she?'

She ignored the question. 'We've got a head start on Reid, and we need to make the most of it. But we've also got to meet up with Sam. So when his majesty has finished on the loo, we need to get him in the car and make a move.'

'Do we have to take him? Won't he just be a hindrance?'

'He'll be a pain in the arse. But he's also a trump card if Maggie doesn't cooperate and we need to apply a bit of pressure.'

Elgar said nothing. He knew he wouldn't win the battle, so there was no point arguing. In any case, much as he hated to admit it, Bridget was probably right.

'Besides,' she said, 'he'll be a pain in your arse, not mine.'

* * *

Beth was silent as they drove. She sat in the left-hand back seat, her magazines on her lap, sometimes looking through them, but more often staring out of her window. Occasionally Maggie would adjust the mirror to check on her. At one point the girl seemed to have fallen asleep, but the next time Maggie checked she was awake and busy plaiting the hair of the princess doll from *Frozen*.

After nearly three hours of driving, Maggie pulled off the motorway. It felt like an achievement to have made it this far without some police car tearing up the road behind them with blue lights flashing. It was cross-country from now on. The girl hadn't said a thing, but Maggie needed a comfort break and an injection of caffeine. As luck would have it, a lay-by, populated by half a dozen lorries and a caravan serving food, came into view. No CCTV here. No ANPR. Despite the change of number plates, she felt that discovery could be just round the corner. She parked and the two of them headed for a dirty grey building which apparently housed toilets. Inside it proved more sanitary than she had feared.

The man and woman in the caravan both spoke with cheerful Yorkshire accents, and when Maggie opted for a bacon and egg roll and a cup of coffee, Beth said she would have the same except she'd rather have an orange juice. She smiled at them with all the skill of a practised charmer and when the woman brought the rolls to them at their red plastic table, Beth was rewarded with a bag of sweets which the woman produced from the pocket of her apron. 'Special treat, love. On the house.'

'Thank you kindly,' the girl replied, the words gleaned from one of her cartoon fantasies.

The woman grinned with delight and turned towards Maggie. 'Ah, your daughter's a real sweetie, isn't she?'

'This is delicious, Mother,' Beth said, moments after swallowing her first bite of bacon, tomato sauce and bread. 'Thank you so much!'

Maggie frowned at the ridiculous accent. But underneath she was beaming with absolute delight. She wanted to jump up and dance a jig. She wanted to sing an Abba solo very badly, at the top of her voice. Most of all, she wanted to hug the girl and never let her go. 'Mother!' The word and the way the girl had said it made tears brim in her eyes. How could Sam not want to look after the child?

Back in the car, as Beth sat quietly in her own world, Maggie found herself thinking about her own father. Ever since Sam had smashed her mobile, she had tried to put him out of her mind. What Sam had done made sense. They had kidnapped her father as a way of forcing her to cooperate, but the fact was that her father's life was drawing to an end anyway. She knew that the relentless creep of dementia could have only one outcome. Already his life was poorer than it ought to be. How aware was he of what was happening to him now? Was he worried about her, or was he happily oblivious inside his own cocooned world? Perhaps he wasn't much different from Beth in the back of the car, content with the here and now and vaguely excited by the unexpected things that were happening to her. Except of course, she told herself savagely, Beth had lost her mother and was desperate to hang onto whatever replacement mother turned up — in this case herself.

Maggie wanted to hang onto her father too. He had been a good and supportive one, especially during and after her mother's slow death from ovarian cancer. She owed him so much. She couldn't just leave him to his captors. Maybe when they realised he wasn't the bargaining counter they had hoped he would be, they would turn him out of their car somewhere and leave him to be rescued by a passer-by. Or maybe not.

She shivered. Back in the real world, a lorry hooted at her for some reason or other. She pressed her horn and held it for a couple of seconds. If Beth hadn't been in the car, she would probably have sworn violently.

She released the horn and with it some of her anger. Not that it was anger which had gripped her, it was fear. It had coiled itself round her as tight as a boa constrictor. Who was she kidding? They wouldn't just let her dad go. Of course they wouldn't. They would kill him and dump his body some place where it would never be found.

* * *

It was going to be one of those days when absolutely nothing went right. The quagmire of depression was sucking Reid into its depths even before they arrived outside Sinead Parkinson's flat. When she failed to respond to her bell, it only confirmed his negative thoughts.

'Doesn't look like her car is here either. She could be anywhere.'

Reid tightened his jaw. Ashcroft was a past master at stating the bloody obvious.

He looked around. There was a woman coming up the path to the flats. Dark grey three-quarter-length coat, matching grey scarf, white hair, flat black shoes.

Red waited until she was near. 'Excuse me, madam. Do you live here?'

She looked him up and down. 'I do.'

'So you know Sinead. Got a little boy and—'

'Course I do. I know everyone in the flats. I make it my business to. The boy stays with me sometimes, watches TV.'

'You don't happen to know where she is?'

'If she's not in, she's out.' She laughed, evidently pleased with her quip.

'Do you know where she works?'

'Course I do. The Jubilee Hotel. Straight out of town. Past an Esso station on the left. Under the railway bridge, then first right. Keep going and you'll see it on the left just past the church.'

'Thank you.'

'Mind you, this isn't one of her normal working days.'

'Oh.'

'Not that there's a normal working week any more, is there? She's on a zero hours contract. Ridiculous if you ask me. How can you know where you are if you don't have regular working hours? Mind you, her mum is a brilliant grandmother. Always having Jake for the day or after school or to stay the night. So if I was you, I'd try the hotel and after that I'd try asking her mother. She lives in Airdale Street.'

Reid thanked her and headed back down the path, muttering. 'Wish I was on a zero hours contract,' he said, as he slumped back into the car. 'At least I'd get paid for every damned hour I work.'

The hotel was only ten minutes away by car, down a narrow lane pockmarked with even more holes than the norm.

Inside it was quiet. Ashcroft and Reid walked over to the reception desk, where a man in a white shirt and black tie was bidding goodbye to a customer. His name badge proclaimed him to be Pavel. 'Can I help you, sir?' he said to Reid.

Ashcroft answered. 'We need to speak to one of your staff, Sinead Parkinson.'

'She's not due in today,' Pavel stated.

'Then we'll speak to the manager,' Ashcroft snarled, as if a receptionist could not possibly answer their questions adequately. He took his role as enforcer pretty seriously. Not that Reid minded. If you owned a dog, you might as well let it have a good bark occasionally.

The manager was a thick-set black-haired man with a moustache. He smelled of cigarette smoke. 'I ask her to work today. We have a conference. But she texts me and says she cannot because it is half-term.' He raised his eyes theatrically. 'She says she is short of money. I offer her extra work. It is arranged. First she says she can. Later she says no!'

'When did she tell you she couldn't work?' Reid said quietly.

'This morning, very early. I tell you. No warning at all!'

When they went outside again it had started to rain, but Reid barely noticed.

'So what made her cry off work this morning?' It was a rhetorical question. Reid was venting his thoughts and his frustration, nothing more.

Ashcroft seemed to understand. 'Why don't we try the grandmother? She might know. Maybe they've all gone on a day trip. It's half-term this week. We could check with the neighbours.'

They did check with the neighbours because when they hammered on Mrs Parkinson's door, there was no reply.

At the fourth attempt they struck lucky. A young woman with bleached hair and a baby slung across her chest answered the door. She introduced herself as Amy.

'We're looking for a Mrs Parkinson. She's not in and we were hoping to speak to her.'

'Ooh! Done something naughty, has she?' Amy laughed. The idea of Mrs Parkinson doing something criminal was clearly far too much of a leap to be credible.

She pushed forward past the men and scanned up and down the street.

'No sign of her car. Must be out.'

'It's actually her daughter, Sinead, that we need to locate.'

'Sinead!' Another laugh. 'Now that I can believe. Sinead and her mother are like chalk and cheese.'

Amy went back inside her house and the men followed.

'Sorry, I just need to put the baby down while she's asleep.' She ran up the narrow stairs and was back down again within a minute.

'I've had a thought,' she said before either of the detectives could ask any more questions. 'Betty, that's Sinead's mother, she was telling me the other day how she hoped to take her grandson to the zoo. Maybe that's where they've gone.'

'Maybe we've struck lucky,' Ashcroft said. They were back in their car and the rain had almost ceased.

'Maybe.' Reid still wasn't in the mood to take anything for granted. 'No news on Sinead's car, I presume?'

At that precise moment, Ashcroft's mobile rang. He listened, grunted a couple of times and hung up.

'Good news, sir. Her car was flagged on a camera heading south out of town about half an hour ago. That's the road you'd take to get to the zoo.'

'And any number of other places too.' Reid's cynicism, honed over years of service, was coming to the fore.

'You'd head west if you were going to pick up the motorway. And the zoo is only five miles away. It's got to be a good bet.'

Reid sighed. 'Alright then, we'll go there.'

* * *

Maggie navigated her way to the village without making a single mistake. She had a good memory when it came to that sort of thing. If she had once driven a route — it wasn't the same when she was a passenger — the detail of roads, turns, bridges, odd landmarks and the like became imprinted in her brain. She liked to think she had her own GPS installed within her skull, which gathered and stored geographical data for future use.

She had driven Ellie there just that once. Ellie had been pregnant and prone to sudden puking and they had stayed in a two-bedroom stone cottage which overlooked

127

the village, a five-minute stroll from the Kings Arms with its blazing fire, suspicious locals and stolid pub food. So when she came to the crossroads known locally as Dead Man's Cross, she felt a shiver of delight run down her spine. This was where the gibbet had been erected in days long past, where many a sheep rustler had breathed his — and in one case her — last. There was no gallows now, of course, only a grassy mound on which a small stone obelisk had been erected to mark the spot for posterity and perhaps as a warning to the visitors who came here in their ridiculously large town cars and with their sheep-chasing dogs. But it wasn't this gory piece of local history which had caused Maggie to shiver. It was the signpost itself, which stood modestly opposite the obelisk and indicated politely that she was a mere two miles from her destination if only she would take the left-hand turn. She felt a surge of pride. She had made it! She had found her way to her destination without a single wrong turn.

The lane which led up to the village was narrow, but thankfully she met no other vehicle coming the other way. She passed two walkers in matching ultramarine anoraks labouring up the gradient, but apart from them, there was nothing to distract her from the notion that she had gone back several years in time. In the passenger seat a bilious Ellie had exclaimed, 'Christ, I think I'm going to wet myself!'

Ellie wasn't with her, but her baby was. Maggie glanced over her left shoulder. Beth was looking out of the window, a look of excitement and expectancy on her face. Maggie suddenly realised that the girl had been here before. She recognised it. Ellie must have brought her.

'Almost there,' Maggie said. She waited for a response but no answer came.

* * *

The zoo car park was filling up fast. Cars were disgorging over-excited children and under-excited adults, all heading for the entrance.

'Let's get on with it,' Reid said. 'And let's hope they did come here.'

They worked methodically, starting at the far side where the earlier arrivals would have parked and checking number plates as they made their way along each row. It wasn't a difficult task, but Reid was in a hurry and he was half tempted to offer a tenner to a random teenager if they found Sinead's car. He didn't of course. It wouldn't take them more than fifteen minutes to cover all the cars.

In fact it took less than three. At the beginning of the third row, they found Sinead's car.

'Bingo!' Ashcroft said.

'Thank God,' Reid replied.

Soon a message was going out over the zoo's loudspeaker system and within a couple of minutes a sprightly old woman marched up to the customer services desk. A curly-haired boy scampered behind her.

'It's my daughter's car,' she said breathlessly. 'I'm borrowing it for the day. Is there a problem? I parked where I was told to.'

'You are Sinead Parkinson's mother?'

'Yes. Has something happened to her? I only saw her this morning. I'm looking after my grandson. It's half-term you see.'

'Please!' Reid raised his hand as if directing a car to slow to a halt. He showed her his ID card. 'I'm Detective Inspector Reid. Let me assure you that your daughter is fine. But we need to speak to her. Can you tell me where she is today?'

'I don't know.' Mrs Parkinson was still flustered.

'So you're driving her car.'

'Yes. She said she wanted to borrow mine. I think she had quite a long way to drive. My car is more comfortable than hers, so we swapped for the day.'

'Can you just confirm your own registration number, please?'

She recited it.

Red glanced at Ashcroft, who had his notebook out. 'ANPR, Sergeant.'

'Yes, sir.'

* * *

The cottage was exactly as she remembered it. The front door was still painted a pale Cambridge blue. Wild flowers jostled with grasses and weeds in the narrow strip of garden which separated the building from the lane. She eased the car into the parking space just beyond the cottage and turned off the engine.

In the silence which followed, she was suddenly struck by the enormous stupidity of what she had done. As long as she had been driving, she had been able to put off the obvious question. But now that she had got here, it reared up like a gigantic cartoon punctuation mark. Well? What on earth was she going to do next?

Behind her, the rear door clicked open. She turned to see Beth slipping out of the car, her doll in one hand and her pink rucksack in the other. Maggie got out herself. The girl made her way to the square window to the left of the porch. Maggie followed her. The girl stood on tiptoes, doing her best to see inside. Maggie did the same, though not on tiptoes. The cottage looked unoccupied. No newspaper lying on the floral print sofa, no abandoned mug on the coffee table, no items of clothing draped over the back of any chairs.

What now? The question hadn't gone away. But an answer of sorts was right in front of her. Attached to the inside of the window was a small white card announcing that the cottage was available as a holiday let. There was a mobile phone number for enquiries and next to it a name, Mrs Sandra Sidebottom.

* * *

Sandra Sidebottom lived in the village and within five minutes she was marching up the lane like a sergeant major leading a platoon of recruits, arms pumping like pistons. She was older than Maggie, late forties maybe, but she was lean and exuded energy, the sort of woman who thought racing up to the top of the local peaks was fun with a capital 'F.'

'You've struck lucky,' she said. 'Someone cancelled a few days ago, so the cottage is available for the next ten days if you are interested.'

'I came here several years ago,' Maggie said, trying to make a bond.

'Before my time, dear.' But Mrs Sidebottom wasn't looking at her. She was scrutinising Beth.

'What's your name, girlie?'

'Beth.'

'You've been here before, haven't you? I never forget a face, not me. Not so long ago with your mum.'

Beth nodded. Her eyes were wary and she looked at Maggie for reassurance.

'So who are you?' Sidebottom said. She put her hands on her hips as if to make clear that she needed an answer before she could possibly allow them into the property.

'I'm an old friend of her mother, Ellie. She's away on business, so we decided to have a little holiday. A sort of spur of the moment thing.'

'I should say.' Sidebottom was still studying Beth as if looking for the answer to the meaning of life.

Finally she turned. 'So, how are you going to pay? I don't have a card machine thingy. We'll have to ring up the agency and for all I know they won't like it and—'

'I can pay cash.' Maggie turned back to the car, grabbed her bag from the passenger footwell and extricated her purse. 'How about two hundred pounds?' she said.

It's amazing what a fistful of cash can do. Mrs Sidebottom's reluctance evaporated. She took the money, counted it and thrust it into the pocket of her padded jacket. She fished out a key and led the way in.

'So that's it, then. The beds are made up. There's kindling and logs round the back for the wood burner. I'll come back in a few minutes and bring you some groceries to keep you going. No extra charge. After that, I run a little store out of the back of the pub. You can call round any time you need something.'

'Is there any paperwork to sign?'

Sidebottom smiled. 'No need, darling. It just complicates things.'

* * *

Reid was just two bites into his very late breakfast — a large bacon sandwich washed down by a takeaway cup of heavily sugared coffee — when Ashcroft's mobile rang. Reid kept chewing. It had been a long wait and he had no intention of not enjoying his breakfast to the full. Even so he watched with anticipation as Ashcroft, who had just stuffed a huge wedge of oversized burger into his mouth, sprayed bits of it across his side of the table while trying to speak coherently into the phone. Ashcroft nodded and grunted, grunted again and nodded more, and finally hung up. On the verge of choking, he took a slug of his tea before swallowing the rest of his mouthful.

'Bingo!' he said, grinning inanely across at his boss. 'Got the mother's car. North Yorkshire. Headed into the moors. Not many cameras there, but there aren't too many roads either.' He stood up and stuffed the rest of his breakfast inside a paper napkin.

Reid snarled, 'Sit down, man. I'm going to finish my breakfast in peace first. Then we'll go.'

* * *

The urge to ring her father had been growing inside Maggie all the way up to North Yorkshire. She knew it would be a risk. Once her phone was turned on, there was the possibility — more of a probability really — that they would track the signal and come running. She could try and keep it short, switch on the mobile, make the call and then power off. If she kept it brief, maybe the risk of being traced wouldn't be so great. She hoped so. She wasn't really sure about the technical side of it.

But the real question was this: what on earth was she going to say to her father, or indeed to the bastards who had kidnapped him? She knew what they wanted. They wanted the evidence which Ellie had had. Evidence which Ellie had almost certainly hidden up here, either in this cottage or somewhere nearby. Why else would Ellie have sent her that cryptic message? But Ellie was dead now. Not an accidental hit-and-run and maybe not even suicide. One night Ellie had got into a big car with opaque windows and had never come home. She had disappeared from the face of the world. Not a single mention on the internet of any suicide. Murdered, and dumped where she would never be found.

And now they were after her and Beth. Because they wanted to know what she knew. Because she and Ellie had once been thick as thieves. They wanted her to lead them to whatever it was that Ellie had died for. Except that she didn't know what that was.

And what then? Even if she knew, and handed it over, would they let her and Beth go? Maybe. Or maybe not. She shuddered.

'Mother.' Beth had appeared in the doorway. 'Can we go out and have an explore? It's nice and sunny now.'

'Why not?' She smiled at the girl and eased herself off the sofa. 'I'll make us a picnic. It'll be fun.'

She went through to the little kitchen to see what she could rustle up. Mrs Sidebottom had dropped some food in as promised: ham and cheese rolls, bags of crisps, some apples and cereal bars. It was a feast. She went through the cupboards. Someone had left a packet of ginger biscuits and a fancy-looking bag of popcorn. There was a flask too.

They would need some water to drink. Now that Beth had suggested it, she found herself desperate to get out of the cottage. Inside, they would be trapped if anything happened. Outside, at least she had the advantage of having been there before. She knew the way to the old quarry. There was a small lake there. It was a great place to picnic and, if necessary, to hide.

* * *

Arthur hadn't spoken a single word since breakfast, not since he had asked the little ferret of a man what his name was. He had forgotten straight away. Something musical, he thought, but he really couldn't remember. He had always had trouble with names and it was a lot worse now. But he did know that he really didn't like these people. Actually the man wasn't too bad. But the woman was two-faced, one minute speaking ever so patronisingly to him, as if he were a complete idiot, and the next telling the man that she didn't want to leave "loose ends." He wasn't sure what she meant by that, but he sensed that it wasn't a good thing.

They were driving north. He knew that because when the sun shone, it was behind them. He wanted to ask them to stop so that he could spend a penny, but he had decided not to speak at all. He knew he needed to make a plan and playing dumb was all he could come up with for now. He wanted them to think he was completely incapable of doing anything for himself. Then maybe they would get careless and he would get a chance to escape. Quite where he would escape to, he really didn't know. He guessed he would have to find somewhere to hide and then hope that someone nice came and found him.

The man turned around from the front seat. 'Are you all right, Arthur?' The car had stopped. They were in a car park and people were walking past.

Arthur said nothing.

'Do you want to go to the toilet? Would you like a sandwich? Or a hamburger? Drink of tea or coffee?'

Arthur frowned and said nothing. The man was actually quite nice.

'We'll have to take it in turns,' the woman said. 'Or he'll go wandering off and we'll never find him.'

* * *

They were heading north still. Arthur was feeling uncomfortable. He hadn't moved from the back seat since they had set out after breakfast. He shut his mind to his discomfort and nibbled at his sandwich. Cheese and lettuce, the man had said. He liked cheese, especially cheddar, but he wasn't so keen on lettuce. Cheese and tomato would have been better, but he wasn't going to complain. He wasn't going to say anything. He really should have told them that he needed to go to the toilet, but he had a plan and he was going to stick to it. As long as he was sitting down, he could hold it in.

The odd thing was that the scenery was familiar. He felt as if he had been here before, in the past, when Maggie had been a kid and before that too. Holidays. That was it. Family holidays in North Yorkshire. Him and Maggie and his beloved Peggy.

'Here. Turn left,' said the man. The woman was called Bridget. He could remember her name, but not the man's. Something odd. Something to do with music. But he just couldn't remember it.

They were bumping along a farm track. There were hedges either side, and through them he could see fields of grass.

'There they are.'

'I'm not blind,' Bridget snapped.

They lurched on, faster than before, and then jerked to a halt.

The man waiting for them was very tall with scruffy hair. He didn't seem to have shaved for several days. The woman was smarter and much prettier, wearing a black leather jacket, jeans and brown boots.

'Just give me a few seconds,' Bridget said.

She didn't say what she needed a few seconds for. She was scrabbling around in her large handbag. Arthur wondered if she wanted to check her lipstick. Peggy had always checked her lipstick before meeting people.

The man with the musical name got out and walked up to the other one. He shook hands with him and then the woman. The two men started to talk. He couldn't hear them that well. He thought the woman looked a bit irritated. Maybe they were talking about football.

Arthur assumed Bridget had finished doing her face because she got out of the car.

'Hi there. You must be Sinead,' she said in her cheerful Irish accent.

'Yes,' replied the woman.

Arthur didn't try and get out of the car, even though his bladder was full to bursting. But he saw it all. It happened as if in a dream, all in slow motion. The woman in brown boots lifted her hand as if to shake hands with Bridget. Bridget lifted her hand too, but there was something in it. A gun with a long black attachment on the end of the barrel — a silencer. Which was why Arthur never heard the shot. He saw the woman's mouth open, he saw a bright red spot appear in the middle of her forehead and he saw her fall backwards. And then he started to urinate.

* * *

Maggie watched in amazed delight. Beth was running ahead like a dog let off the leash. If Maggie had thought about it at all, she might have realised that after two days of being cooped up in hotels and cars, a child would have bundles of energy to burn.

Maggie wanted to return to the old disused quarry where she and her parents had spent many happy days in her childhood. Ellie and she had swum in the lake in the quarry more than once. Happy memories from the time before things had gone wrong.

Running on ahead, Beth was like a hound following a scent. The track had several forks in it and each time they reached one, Beth seemed to know instinctively which turn to take. Maggie remembered it as her father had taught her: first left, then right, then left again, and so on until you reached the top of the incline.

'Beat you!' the girl said, whirling round, arms stretched up to the heavens. The clouds were racing across the blue sky like ethereal chariots. 'I'm the queen of the castle and you're the dirty rascal!'

Maggie couldn't answer. She had made it to the top, but only just. She bent forward, hands on knees, sucking in air and trying to regain her breath. She was hopelessly overweight and unfit. She was also wearing totally unsuitable footwear. She had completely forgotten to bring trainers or indeed any footwear at all that didn't have a ridiculous heel. She was saddled with her short brown fashion boots.

'Mum was a really good runner,' Beth said. 'I'm quite good too. We went on a charity run last year. It was really fun.'

Maggie straightened up and tried to smile, but her ribs were hurting, so she suspected it was more of a grimace. 'I can see you are,' she said. She could also see — though she kept it to herself — that if she wanted to take Ellie's place and be Beth's 'mother,' then she was always going to be compared and she would often be found wanting.

Maggie began to take in the panorama, soaking up memories and scenery. She looked back down to the village and was surprised at how far they had come and how quickly. She rotated slowly, taking in the grass and the crags and the scattered sheep. Finally her eyes alighted on the quarry. It didn't seem to have changed much. More greenery on the slopes, more bushes, but otherwise just as she remembered. A tempting (but bitterly cold) lake in the centre of the quarry floor, old buildings which had long been stripped of their machinery and a metal gantry on which she had once climbed (much to her mother's horror). High above, a pair of large birds hovered. Maggie thought they might be buzzards. Her father would have known.

She felt anxiety and guilt wrench at her. Perhaps she should have rung him? Perhaps she should have thrown herself upon their mercy, given them everything they wanted and hoped they took pity. Perhaps, perhaps, perhaps. Her thoughts ran wild around the inside of her skull. *You've abandoned him. After all he did for you, you gave up on him.* The voices of self-doubt and criticism wailed like banshees. She shook her head, stretched her neck and tried to concentrate on the here and now.

'Race you to the bottom!' Beth grinned up at her and then with a whoop she began to run.

'Careful!' Maggie called, but the girl was gone. *Careful*: what any parent would have said as their beloved ran headlong down a rough incline. Her mother especially . . . Her poor mother. The memory was as sharp as if it had only been yesterday. She was lying in bed in the hospice, her face little more than a skull with the skin stretched taut across the bones. 'You will look after Dad, won't you? Promise me you will.' But how could she look after her father now?

She turned and followed Beth, walking as fast as she could manage in her silly heels. One thought overwhelmed all the others. Whatever else, she could keep Beth safe.

* * *

'Hell, it doesn't half stink in here.' Sam was sitting in the front passenger seat, having argued that his legs were far too long for the back. It was the first thing anyone had said since they had started off ten minutes previously, just after they had disposed of Sinead's naked body at the bottom of a slurry pit.

They were all crammed into Sinead's mother's car, having hidden Bridget's car behind a disused farm building. Eventually someone would be deputed to pick it up and bring it in and no doubt the first thing that person would do would be to open all four windows. Arthur's pent-up urine had soaked a huge area of the back seat.

But Arthur was still with them, and so were his trousers and pants and the stench of urine. Elgar was only too well aware of this because it was he who had been consigned to the back seat, right next to Arthur. He didn't resent it as much as he should have. He was used to being last. He had always been shorter than the other boys in his class. He had been rubbish at sport, lower-middle in the brain department and to cap it all he had a surname beginning with the letter 'Z.'

'Why the hell didn't you make him pee at the services?' It was Sam again. He would have been a cocky bastard at school. Elgar knew the type. Taller, more confident and cleverer. A charmer of teachers. Not like Elgar.

'We asked him, but he just sat in the car with that blank look on his face.'

'Doesn't he ever talk, then?'

'Barely.'

Elgar wound his window down further and tried to imagine he was somewhere else. Arthur began to hum a tune which Elgar recognised but couldn't identify. Bridget hooted at some driver who had offended her. Sam was rocking very slightly in his seat, backwards and forwards.

'Did you really need to shoot her?' Elgar was caught off-balance by Sam's sudden question. Sam was looking fixedly at Bridget and had stopped rocking.

Bridget continued to look ahead. 'I was obeying orders,' she said.

'That's what they said at Nuremberg.'

Bridget's hand hit the horn again. There was a lorry in front, but it wasn't going slowly. Elgar slipped his hand inside his jacket, feeling for his gun. Where was this conversation going to end up? If Sam was spoiling for a fight, he was certainly making all the right moves.

Bridget answered with exaggerated calm. Elgar recognised the danger signs. 'We all obey orders. You know that.'

'She's got a kid.'

'She was unreliable. We're trying to protect you. Or have you forgotten?'

'She trusted me,' Sam said. 'She came and rescued me.'

'You used her, Sam. Let's not get all sentimental. Sooner or later she would have realised her folly and she would have betrayed you. She would have betrayed Bowman too.'

Elgar closed his eyes momentarily. In an ideal world, he would have sided with Sam. But Bridget's brutal logic was compelling. After all, this was the world they had all chosen to live in. He hadn't been the one who pulled the trigger, but that didn't make him innocent. He had known that it was bound to happen. If he had really wanted to, he could have tried to stop it.

* * *

'Left here.'

Bridget had paused briefly at a crossroads. There was a large piece of stone set on a grass-covered mound. Elgar noticed it and marked it in his head. Might be useful if Bowman needed directions.

Elgar was directing them courtesy of the tablet he had on his lap. The tracker was embedded in a piece of jewellery which the unfortunate Sinead had given to the little girl. And it was leading them unerringly to their destination. 'Couple of miles at most,' he said, trying to put Sinead out of his mind.

Two miles later they were in and almost immediately through the village, the only building of interest being a pub.

'That's the car,' Sam said. They were the first words he had spoken for some time.

'Are you sure?'

Bridget stopped the car and got out. Sam followed her over to the car and they peered in. 'She's changed the plates,' he said, 'but that's definitely the car.'

Bridget walked back and opened the door of their car. Elgar sat squinting at the tiny screen. 'So where are they?' she said.

'Out there somewhere.' He flicked a finger towards the moors beyond the end of the road.

'Right,' Bridget said. 'Let's go and get it done.' She walked to the boot and removed a small carry-bag which she slung over her shoulder. 'Come on, Arthur. We're going for a walk.'

Arthur was already out of the car. He had walked over to the house and was touching the blue front door as if he was a ghost hunter trying to locate a presence.

'So what's the plan?' Sam said, pulling on a jacket. 'Just so as I know.'

Bridget looked into his face. 'You stay here, Samuel. That's the plan.'

'What are you talking about?'

'Orders,' Bridget said. 'The boss should be here very soon. You can bring him up to date. Make him a cup of tea.'

Elgar watched Sam and wondered if he was going to dig in his heels and if so how they were going to deal with it. It was a small place, but people lived here. You kill someone in a place like this and people see and remember. It was much easier operating in a large anonymous city.

'If you harm even a single hair on the kid's head,' Sam was saying, 'I'll kill you.'

For a few moments the two of them became animals facing off. Bridget was the attack dog and Sam the stag. Elgar watched without a flicker of an eyelid. His eyes were trained on Sam, poised to intervene if he reacted. He knew Sam only by reputation and from reading the files, but that didn't cover a situation like this. He lifted his hand, ready to pull his gun if he needed to.

Bridget gave the shortest of laughs. 'Jesus, Sam, I'm a Catholic. What do you take me for?'

Sam didn't answer. He chewed on his lower lip for several more moments before giving a sudden shrug. He stuck his hands into his pockets. 'OK.'

'We shouldn't be too long. Anyway, you hold the fort here.' Bridget gestured towards Arthur, who had started plodding off up the track which led into the hills. 'I reckon the old man knows the cottage, and it looks like he knows the way to the quarry too. We'll see you later.'

She headed off after Arthur. Elgar followed. He felt exposed. He had a horror of being shot in the back and he didn't feel comfortable until they were some distance from Sam. They had frisked him earlier, after Sinead's death. They had apologised as they did it, because he was meant to be on the same side as them, but neither of them had wanted to take any chances. One thing Elgar and Bridget were agreed on was that you never know what people are capable of until they have done it. And then it's too late.

* * *

Despite her best efforts to keep up with Beth, Maggie trailed in a distant second in their race to the quarry. She arrived panting like an overweight labrador. Beth was sitting cool and unconcerned against the circular stone archway of the old lime kiln. She was chewing on an apple while she surveyed the contents of her rucksack, which she had laid out on a slab of stone in front of her.

From what Maggie's father had told her, the quarry had fallen out of use during the Second World War. Too far away from any railway lines or proper roads, it had never been resurrected, despite the influx of returning soldiers who needed employment. Instead, Mother Nature had reclaimed the area for herself. The single row of miners' cottages had lost their long slate roof. The working innards of the kilns and other industrial buildings had been ripped out during the war and transported away, the metal being recycled into munitions for the military. For some reason, a single gantry had been left standing.

'Shall we have our picnic?' Beth's display of items included the rolls and other goodies which the two of them had assembled from the supplies provided by Mrs Sidebottom.

Maggie croaked a feeble 'yes,' and slumped down against the other side of the archway. She downed several gulps of water and then began to eat her own packed lunch, forcing herself to do so methodically and slowly. 'If you want to lose weight,' she had been told, 'you need to eat less food and if you want to eat less food you need to eat more slowly. That way your stomach will have time to tell you it is full before you stuff it to bursting.' Maggie had nodded sagely at the skinny health worker, but she rarely followed her advice. Today, however, she had another reason to eat slowly. She was trying to think.

'I expect the lake is very cold,' the girl said. She had already finished eating and was packing all her things away with great care. The last item was a little square box, painted various shades of pink and white with a ballerina on the lid. She took a little bracelet out of it and put it on her wrist. It was pretty. It reminded Maggie of a bracelet which she had been given as a child but had managed to lose. Maggie watched her in fascination and something akin to motherly love swelled up inside her.

'The lake is always very cold.' Maggie had skinny-dipped in it more than once, but said, 'It is very dangerous for swimming.' Maggie felt even more like a mother as she said this. Serious and protective.

'So what shall we do?'

'Why don't we hunt for treasure?'

The girl frowned and then Maggie did too. Perhaps Beth was too old for treasure hunts. When did little girls become too big for such things? She really didn't know. After all, she wasn't a real mother.

Beth stood up and walked towards Maggie until she was up close. 'Mother,' she said in the sort of hushed voice that girls use when they are telling secrets, 'do you know something?'

Beth paused. Later Maggie would think of it as a pregnant pause, bulging with meaning, the moment when anything and everything became possible. But at the time it was just a pause. 'Mum hid some treasure here.'

* * *

Arthur knew the place where he was going to die. Most days, he couldn't remember what he had eaten for breakfast — or even if he had had breakfast at all. He couldn't currently remember the name of the town where he lived. But the odd thing was he knew the place they had brought him to. In fact the whole area felt familiar. As he had looked around and smelled the air, memories had come bubbling up to the surface. He had come on holiday here with his parents, more than once. They had brought the caravan — lime green and beige with its comforting smell of damp bedding and bacon. A man with a bushy beard had let them stay in a field at the back of his house. There had been an outside tap and a long green hose so they could always get water and the woman used to sell them eggs laid by her brown hens. He had brought Peggy and Maggie here too. They had stayed in a cottage. Peggy wasn't the camping type, but she had loved the cottage and she seemed happier here than she had ever been at home.

They used to walk too. Peggy had been less keen than him, but she never said 'no,' even when Maggie came along just when they had all but given up on the idea that they would ever have a baby. That next summer, they had walked to the top of the peak which overlooked the quarry, Maggie on his back in a baby carrier. There they had promised to be the happiest family ever — tempting fate. It was six months before the cancer diagnosis. The doctors had done their best, but the treatment wasn't so effective in those days and Peggy had passed silently away one afternoon, leaving a giant hole which had never been filled.

So as he walked on up through the grass slopes, heading for the quarry where so many memories still resided, he thought it was fitting that his life's journey would end in this place. Soon he and Peggy would be together again.

He knew he was about to die. He had seen Bridget shoot the blonde woman. He knew what she was capable of. 'No loose ends,' she had said to the little man with the musical name. It hadn't sounded good.

At the top Arthur stopped and turned round. Bridget and the man were close behind, walking in single file. They caught up with him and they too paused, staring down the hill into the quarry.

'Come on, Arthur,' the woman said. 'Nearly there.'

* * *

Beth led the way with her pink rucksack. 'Explorers must carry everything they need,' she said. 'Because you never know.'

The quarry comprised three levels, and the place where they had eaten their picnic was in the middle. They walked west at first. To their right were the remains of various buildings, home now to grass, weeds and a few gorse bushes, and beyond these a sheer, heavily mined cliff face. To the left there was nothing. Some thirty metres below was a large hollow, three-quarters filled by a lake of still water off which the afternoon sun reflected, slashing into Maggie's eyes when she was stupid enough to look into it. Mostly she concentrated her gaze on Beth, monitoring her progress like a mother duck giving a duckling the lead for the first time. Beth walked with swinging arms and head held high. She seemed too sensible for her years. 'Don't go near the edge, Mother,' she had instructed Maggie, as if she were the adult. 'It's dangerous.'

Eventually they came to a steep incline and now Beth began to scramble upwards. The path she took had once been a stairway, cut into the turf and rock, but this was hardly discernible now and as Maggie followed she found her feet slipping and twisting on the uneven surface. At the top, Beth stopped and waited for Maggie to catch up.

She was standing in front of a terrace of four miners' cottages.

'Do you want to look for it yourself, or shall I show you?'

Maggie was panting again, taking in huge gulps of air. 'You show me,' she managed to say.

The girl walked along the front of the terrace until she reached the fourth door.

'I think this is the right one.' She stood at the entrance. Maggie looked inside. She could see a number of tiles scattered over what had once been a floor. She didn't think there was a risk of anything falling on their heads, but she couldn't be sure. 'Be very careful, Beth. Watch where you are putting your feet.'

The girl took this advice seriously, making her way one step at a time across the room to the far side. 'In here,' she said, pointing to an old stove. She grabbed the handle and pulled without success. 'It's stuck,' she said.

Maggie bent down and grabbed it herself. She tugged hard. Nothing happened. As a schoolgirl, the only sport she had been any good at was the shot-put. She had once been strong, the first person to be called on when something immovable needed shifting. But the toned muscles had long since gone. She grunted and tried again.

Nothing. She felt frustration rising within her. She had to get inside the damned thing. She had to know what Ellie had died for. She sucked in a deep breath and twisted again, pressing down with her weight — she had enough of that, after all. For a second or two there was not even a hint of movement and then — bang! — the handle slammed down. She pulled and this time the door opened. It wasn't a treasure box like Beth had in her bag, but a dirty little newspaper package. She ripped open the paper. Inside there was another layer, of bubble wrap. She opened that too. Inside that — Maggie had a ridiculous flashback to games of pass the parcel at birthday parties — was a small white paper package. And inside that, finally, a memory stick.

'Is that it?' There was obvious disappointment in Beth's voice. What had she been expecting? Pieces of eight? A ruby ring? A crown fit for a princess? *Probably*.

'I'm afraid so.' Maggie went outside and walked to the end of the terrace, where she shrugged off her rucksack and knelt down in the shade. She got out a thin rectangular case, unzipped it and took a small tablet from it. Beth followed her, but turned away, apparently bored with treasure hunting.

It didn't take Maggie long to get the tablet up and running. She inserted the memory stick and waited. She glanced up. She didn't want the child watching over her shoulder. Who knew what horrors there might be on it?

But Beth's attention was elsewhere. She was standing motionless, looking down at the quarry basin below.

'Mother,' she said.

Maggie ignored her. She had just opened the first of the many files on the memory stick. This one was a photograph. An old one from pre-digital days, it was grainy and hard to make out. But it was a photograph of a child.

'Mother!' This time there was an edge of anxiety in her voice. 'Mother! There are some people down below.'

* * *

Arthur had no doubt that this was the place. The lime kiln, the lake and the path they had taken, all this and everything else he could see tallied exactly with what he remembered. It all seemed part of a different life — life before Peggy's death. He had never come back, afraid it would cause him too much pain. This was their place. Yet coming back now didn't bring back pain or sadness, only pleasure.

'They're up there,' someone said.

He looked up and saw two figures standing in front of the old miners' houses. A woman and a child. For a moment he thought the child was Maggie, but the hair was all wrong, too short. He looked at the adult. That *was* Maggie! Confusion engulfed him. Maggie? What was she doing here? And who was the child? Did Maggie have a child? She'd never told him she had a child, he was sure of that. Did he have a grandchild? He felt faint. His head was swirling.

'Hello, Maggie!' The Irish woman was shouting up at them. What was her name? Bridie? Bernadette? Something like that.

'We've got your father here, safe and sound. All we want is for you to cooperate and then you can take him home!'

Maggie didn't reply. He could see her pulling a black rucksack onto her back. The child had a little pink one and was doing the same. It must be a girl. He wondered what her name was.

'If you don't, I'll shoot him!'

Maggie had bent down now and was talking to the little girl.

'I am not bluffing, Maggie!' The woman shouted louder this time, but he sensed no emotion in her voice. Arthur didn't like her at all. Bridie, was it? He couldn't dredge the name up. Anyway, he much preferred the man

148

with the musical name. 'I've already killed one person today!' The woman was getting louder and more strident.

Arthur remembered the woman in the brown boots. He remembered how they had stripped her body and then dumped it into the slurry pit.

Bridie — he thought she must be called Bridie — had got the gun in her hand again. She was screwing the silencer onto the end of the barrel.

He watched her do so with curiosity rather than fear. He had seen people do it on TV. Usually the baddie who did this wore black gloves. Bridie's were dark brown.

Arthur turned round. He was standing a few steps away from the edge of the quarry cliff. He looked down. There were more bushes and gorse than he remembered around the lake, but otherwise it hadn't changed. The water was still and inviting, but he remembered how cold it was. He shivered at the thought of it.

It was as if he had come full circle. If the woman shot him now, here, he wouldn't care. It would be karma, fate, what was meant to be. Arthur wasn't a religious man, but he had come to understand that life had its patterns. Dying here would make absolute sense.

'Arthur!' It was the woman again.

He turned. She was barely three paces away and she was now pointing the gun at him. Bridie. No, not Bridie. It seemed ridiculously important to know what her name was before the end. Bridget. That was it! She was Bridget.

'You don't need to shoot me, Bridget, because I'm going to jump,' he told her. He stepped away from her, closer to the edge. This was the only way. He felt calm. Bridget thought she was in control, but that wasn't how he saw it.

She lowered the gun a little. It was pointing lower now. Was she going to shoot him in the legs? He did hope not. Wasn't that what they did in Northern Ireland — kneecapping? Arthur saw Bridget's expression waver. He grinned. It was a small victory.

'Don't be stupid,' the woman said. 'Your daughter is up there. She wants to take you home.'

He laughed. 'My daughter is dead,' he said.

The uncertainty on the woman's face gave way to confusion.

'Your daughter is alive!' The woman spoke loudly, as if to bring him to his senses. 'Look, up there.' She pointed with her gun. 'Come on,' she said, her voice suddenly soft. 'Let's go and see her.' She stepped closer to Arthur and held out her hand, the one without the gun. He edged backwards.

A shadow passed over them, a cloud scurrying across the sun. He glanced up towards Maggie and the girl. Who was that girl?

'Come on, Arthur.' Bridget stepped closer again, arm extended.

He took her hand. 'Thank you,' he said. 'Thank you very much.'

She was a small woman and her hand was small too, but her fingers were talons, designed for seizing prey and tearing it apart. She gripped and pulled. He braced himself, stretching forward his other arm and grabbing at the sleeve of her jacket. He threw his weight backwards. She squealed. He saw her gun slip from her gloved hand and fall noiselessly into a tuft of long grass. A male voice yelled, the music man whose name he would never know. He felt Bridget's free hand scrabbling at his face, her nails cutting into his papery skin. But the pain only spurred him on. He was a heavy man and his two hands clamped round hers were plier-tight. There was a searing pain in his ear. Had she bitten him? He didn't care. Nothing mattered any more. It was just a question of hanging on.

'Dad!' That was Maggie shouting from high above. He could recognise her voice anywhere. He strained as hard as he could. He felt a sudden shift in the equilibrium. He began to fall backwards, out into the void, and where he went the woman inevitably followed. There was a sudden rush of air and a wild screaming in his ear which told him he had done it. It was over.

* * *

One moment her father was standing down below, in full view, tussling with the woman, and then they had both disappeared over the edge and out of sight.

It had all happened so quickly that Maggie found it impossible to believe what she had seen. She felt faint, as if she too might tumble over. Her throat was paralysed, as if it, like her brain, had gone into shock. 'Dad!' she wanted to cry out, but the word never got beyond her lips. She felt a surge of nausea, and bent down low, hands on knees. She vomited and for several seconds she remained doubled over, waiting for it to subside.

'Mother?' Beth tugged at her hand.

She stared blankly at the girl. A few moments before — while they were putting their rucksacks on — she had told Beth what to do if things 'went wrong,' and immediately they had gone disastrously wrong. 'Remember what I said?' she whispered, as if her voice might carry to the man down below them.

The girl nodded.

'Don't look back and don't stop running.'

Down below them the man was standing on the edge of the cliff. He stood still, looking into the quarry, and for a mad moment Maggie imagined that he was going to jump off the cliff too. Then he turned and looked up at her. He pulled out a gun. No silencer on this one.

'Maggie!' he shouted. 'Come down here! Don't do anything stupid.'

Maggie put her hand on Beth's shoulder. 'Remember what I said.' She bent down and kissed the girl on the forehead. At the same time she slipped the memory stick into her hand. 'Don't lose it,' she said. 'Now, run!'

* * *

151

It was several moments before Elgar reacted. That went against all his training and all his experience. But as he peered over the edge of the cliff and saw the two bodies lying spread-eagled on a huge boulder next to the lake, the thought flashed across his brain that this must be a dream. The two bodies were still locked together, the old man's two hands entwined with Bridget's.

He shook his head, trying to clear his confusion. He turned and looked up. Maggie was bending over the child. He shouted something. He wasn't sure what, but he saw them both look at him for an instant and then they both started to run, in opposite directions. Maggie was running westwards. Elgar had no idea what the terrain was like, but as he watched he quickly came to the conclusion that he would be able to catch her. She was overweight. He knew that from all the observation they had carried out back in Oxford. She ran as if running was the most unnatural activity in the world. She was wearing brown boots, not walking boots but fancy fashion boots with a heel. They would, he thought, be the death of her.

He began to jog after her. There was no need to run fast. He could see her in full profile, running down the slope and he was confident that he would soon close the gap. He wondered where she was trying to get to. Just escape, or maybe loop back round to her car. By the time he had got to the end of the quarry, she was only twenty metres or so in front of him. They were on the same level now, both heading down a shallow valley.

It was clear that she was beginning to struggle. Her arms were flailing either side of her like the sails of a demented windmill. It could be only a matter of seconds before she crashed to the ground. She would scrabble desperately back onto her feet, panic rising, and then before she had gone more than a few slithering paces she would slip and fall again to squeal and yell and eventually plead for her life. It would be easy.

But Maggie didn't fall. She slipped once. Her left hand had dipped down to touch the ground, but somehow she was up again and still ploughing on. Elgar began to accelerate. She was moving faster than he thought possible. She reminded him of a rhinoceros. Those big, apparently cumbersome animals could generate quite a speed. Not exactly nought to sixty in ten seconds, but once they reached their top speed, they sure as hell took some stopping.

Elgar didn't panic, nor did he try and run faster. There was no need because he was gaining on her. His feet were moving deftly over the terrain, his trainers stepping expertly from tussock to tussock. The gap between them was closing and her movements were becoming more laboured and jerky. He was not an imaginative man, but he thought he could smell her fear. The ground dropped away in front of her, not sharply, but enough, running from right to left. This was where the water from the higher ground funnelled, turning the ground into a slippery, boggy trap. Elgar could feel the sponginess of the ground beneath his own feet. Sooner or later she would fall down or get stuck in the boggy ground, and then it would only be a matter of seconds before he closed the gap completely. But she was still moving forward. Her progress was increasingly erratic, however, as her stupid heels subsided with every step into the increasingly sodden ground. She was having to pull hard to extricate them and to force herself forwards into further squelching, energy-sapping strides. But she wasn't giving up. Elgar was impressed.

There were bushes scattered across the grassy incline, and it was almost into the middle of one of these that the rhino now blundered. He saw her trip and fall down, briefly out of his sight. He heard her scream of despair. Only now did he quicken his pace.

* * *

What would you do? Maggie's father had loved to play that game, when she and her brother Paul were sufficiently young and biddable. Until Paul, two years younger but wanting to be older, announced one holiday that it was a stupid game and he wasn't playing it any more. And so her father had stopped.

It had been a game they played exclusively when they went on holiday. It had started the time they stayed in a converted windmill, and Paul and she were sleeping in the bedroom at the top. 'How would you escape if the kitchen caught fire in the middle of the night?' her father had asked them over supper, totally straight-faced. The answer they had come up with had been to jump from their one window onto the sail and wait for their weight to turn the sail and bring them close to the earth, and then try and drop into the beech hedge to break their fall. Father had been delighted. Next time it had been, 'What would you do if your mother and I were taken with a sickness that made us both delirious?' which had been a rather unsettling question given that they were staying in a Scottish bothie with a telephone which only received incoming calls. But never in all his 'What would you do?' games had her father asked, 'What would you do if a homicidal psychopath with a gun is pursuing you across unfamiliar terrain far from any visible habitation?'

She knew she couldn't keep running for much longer and she knew the man pursuing her was closing in on her. It was only a matter of time before he caught up with her and killed her. But her father's game — she had never worked out how serious he had been — was like learning to ride a bicycle. Even though she hadn't played it since stroppy little Paul had brought it to an abrupt end, the 'what would you do?' part of her brain kicked into action.

A low bush loomed in front of her. She had been concentrating so hard on staying upright and then looking back to check where the man was that she blundered right into it. Something caught her left foot and she somersaulted through the air, landing on her back. She lay there, looking up into cloudless blue sky. What would you do? What now?

She sensed and then heard him, a staccato laugh. She groaned, half-opening her eyes. 'Help me!' she said pathetically. Another rat-a-tat of laughter. He wasn't a big man, but he was looming over her now, the gun hanging casually in his fingers. 'Daddy,' she moaned. The man bent closer, grinning from one cauliflower ear to the other.

'Daddy?' she said again. She could smell him now. He was close, very close, his breath a mixture of pickled onions and peppermint. She lifted her hand as if to beg for help, until it touched and then gripped the collar of his coat. She swung her other arm harder than she had ever in her life before. The stone she was holding in her cupped palm smacked against his temple. He screamed and pulled away but her fingers, attached to his coat, pulled him back. She struck wildly at him twice more.

Something dropped onto her thigh. His gun! She grabbed it, rolled sideways onto her front and forced herself up onto her knees. She had never fired a gun before, but there was a first time for everything. She pointed it at him and waited for him to lunge at her, but he lay there on his side in the mud, with blood down the side of his head, showing no obvious intention of getting up. He was alive. She could see his chest heaving. A low moan emitted from his mouth. Now was the time to pull the trigger. If she didn't kill him, he would kill her. It was as simple as that. Except that it wasn't. She wasn't a cold-blooded killer. He was the cold-blooded killer. And he was on the ground, whimpering. She rose warily to her feet. She was in charge now. But her thoughts were elsewhere. She needed to get to Beth and then get the two of them out of there pronto. She stared at him. Suppose he was pretending? Maybe he was waiting for an opportunity to hurl himself at her as soon as her guard was down.

She stretched out her arm, tensing it. She wondered how much of a kick the gun would give. The man moaned again, a desperate attempt to enlist her sympathy. She wasn't going to be taken in by that. She pulled the trigger and the gun cracked. She was surprised by how quiet the noise was and how little her hand jumped. The bullet exploded a small stone next to his ear, closer than she had intended. He yelped.

'Take your shoes off,' she ordered.

He looked at her as if she was speaking a language unknown to him. 'Shoes and socks,' she said more loudly, as if turning up the volume would make her more intelligible. She waggled the gun at the central mass of his body.

'Mobile!' she demanded when his feet were bare.

He scrabbled in his pocket and produced one.

Then she told him to shut his eyes, and she pulled the trigger again. This time her aim was better. This time he screamed in agony. She turned southwards and started heading up the slope. She had bought herself time. Beth would be waiting for her at the cottage. That was what they had agreed. Maggie was heaving and puffing. She couldn't run any more, but that didn't matter. She had bought herself plenty of time. There was no way that the man was going to come sprinting after her, not with the big toe missing from his left foot. She turned round to check. The man had made it to his knees, but he was showing no sign of standing up.

She carried on up towards the top of the incline. The gun was still hanging from her right hand. She lifted it up to study it. Guns were not her style. Carry a gun and sooner or later you pull the trigger and kill someone. She paused. Just to the left there was a cleft in the rock. She had no idea how deep it was, but she dropped the weapon into it anyway. Then she continued marching, determined to catch up with Beth.

* * *

Sam was being very odd. He always was, but this time it was different.

Beth had been so pleased to see him when she got to the cottage. He had bent down and given her a big hug and she had told him how Maggie had told her to run back to the cottage and hide upstairs until she came. But now that Sam was there, everything was alright, wasn't it?

'Of course it is,' he had said.

But there was another man in the cottage. He was sitting in the armchair when she arrived. He was a bit like an owl. He had a round face and round thick glasses. He was wearing a dark grey suit and he was pretty fat.

'This gentleman and I need to talk, sweetie,' Sam said, 'so perhaps you can play in your bedroom until we've finished.'

Then he had taken her upstairs.

'You know that I love you more than any other little girl in the whole wide world, don't you?'

She had nodded. It wasn't the first time he had said this. When he did, it usually meant he was going to go away for a while. That was the problem with Sam. He never stayed for long. He was always going away.

* * *

It was only after she had crested the rise and the village had come into view that Maggie's anxieties began to build again. It was a tiny village — God only knew how it managed to support a pub — and there wasn't a single person in sight. There was no sign of Beth, which meant that she must be inside the cottage. Maggie had told her to go upstairs and hide in the wardrobe in the big bedroom. So that is where she would surely be, safe and sound. Maggie dared not think about any alternative.

It was easier going downhill, but she was still panting like an overheated dog. There was a pain in her left calf, perhaps she had pulled a muscle. She walked on as fast as she was able, conscious that if she tripped over and twisted her ankle or anything stupid like that, she would be in even more trouble. She scanned the area as she approached the cottage. She could see her car where she had parked it. There were a couple of other cars parked just beyond the cottage. They must have brought her father in one of them, she guessed.

She told herself not to worry. She had to think. What are you going to do now, Maggie? Beth has the evidence. So find her, get her in the car and get the hell out of the place. Get to somewhere safe (was anywhere safe for her?) and then decide what to do with the memory stick.

* * *

Beth unzipped the small compartment on the back of her rucksack, ferreted around inside it and pulled out a pack of tissues. 'Bless you,' the label said. Her mum had given them to her and she hadn't used a single tissue since. She slipped a finger and thumb inside it and pulled out the memory stick.

It wasn't the treasure she had expected to find, but she wasn't so young or daft that she didn't know what it was. She had her own tablet. Sam had given it to her for Christmas. Her mother hadn't been too keen. 'Where did you get the money for that?' she had snapped. Which was a good question, because whenever Sam turned up he never seemed to have any money to spare.

'It's not brand new,' Sam had replied with a laugh. 'I got it off eBay.' Sam always had an answer.

'Well, I suppose beggars can't be choosers,' her mum had replied and she had pecked him on the cheek.

Beth got her tablet out from under her pillow and opened it up. She plugged the memory stick in and waited. It behaved like an old tablet bought on eBay too, really slow. Her friend Amelia had been given one by her mum's boyfriend. That had come from Argos and it was new and super-fast, but Beth didn't mind too much.

There were lots of different files on the memory stick. Some were much bigger than others. She thought that was because they were different types of files. She had learned about different file types at an after-school club, but she couldn't remember what they all meant. The names weren't very helpful. Mixtures of letters and numbers. Probably the letters stood for something, but she didn't know what.

She paused and listened. She could hear Sam and the man talking downstairs. She was safe. She double-clicked on one of the files and it opened.

It was a photograph. So was the next one and the next one. A mother and a baby. A bigger child on his own. Another child, a bit older. Or maybe it was the same child a bit older. It was hard to tell because the photos were very fuzzy. Perhaps because they were old.

The next photo was much better. Several adults in a group staring at the camera, and one of them, she realised with a shock, was her mother.

She held her breath. It had gone quiet downstairs. Then there was someone else talking, a woman. It sounded like Maggie. She gasped with relief, and then gulped with fear. Maggie must have escaped from the man with the gun, but suppose the fat man wanted to kill her? Would Sam let him? Did Sam have a gun? Thoughts and fears cascaded through her head. Then, suddenly, she heard Sam shouting, 'sweetie!' She didn't like him calling her sweetie, but he often did. He was calling her downstairs. She pulled the memory stick out of her tablet and stuffed it back into the tissues and then back into the rucksack. She snapped the tablet shut and pushed it into the rucksack too. Then she went downstairs to see if it really was Maggie.

* * *

Maggie knew someone was in the cottage. Not just Beth, but someone else. The three pebbles she had left on the stone slab outside the front door had been moved. It could have been Beth, but she saw a footprint where the stones had been and it was much too big to be Beth's. Besides, as she was trudging down the moor towards the house, she had had this overwhelming sense that someone was watching her. It was a sixth sense, a gut feeling. Women's intuition. Whatever it was, she had it in spades.

But she had no option but to go inside. She wasn't going to walk out on the kid. She wasn't going to cut and run. She had done enough of that in the past. She was going to see it through to the end, whatever that end might be. She glanced behind her, up the hill. Her would-be killer was in sight now. He was hobbling. She still had time on her side, but she didn't have forever. She twisted the door handle and went inside.

She saw Sam first. He was standing with his back to the window, his face hidden in shadow, hands dangling. She wasn't sure whether she felt relief or dread.

Then she saw the other man, reclining in the armchair across the other side of the room, and she knew it ought to be dread.

'You must be Maggie,' he said.

'Where's Beth?'

The man smiled. It failed to reassure her. Sitting there in the armchair he looked podgy and unhealthy. But his eyes, grey, unblinking and magnified by the thick lenses of his glasses, were cold and malevolent.

'She's upstairs. She's fine. Best on all counts if she stays there.'

'Says who?' She wasn't going to show him how scared she was.

'Says me.'

'I need to see her.'

'Afterwards.'

After what? After she had 'cooperated?' After she had told him where the memory stick was? What if she refused? What then?

Sam stepped forward. 'Tell you what, Maggs, you sit down.' He lifted his head and shouted up into the ceiling. 'Beth!' A pause while they all listened. A squeak of floorboards. 'Come down for a moment, sweetie.'

He didn't wait for a reply, but took Maggie by the elbow and led her to the sofa. 'Sit, Maggs.' As if she was a dog undergoing training. Maggie's brain was going into freefall. What was this? Sam playing the good cop? And the other guy was the bad cop? He certainly felt like a cop of some sort. Special branch, probably. MI5. The sort of cop who had shadowed them in the protest days. But if that was the case, then who the hell was Sam? Was he one of them? One of the people who had killed Ellie? Was that who he was?

Sam's hand had shifted to her shoulder and was pressing on it hard. She sat down. Her eyes went to the stairs, where Beth's feet had appeared. The feet came down, one cautious step after the other. When her face came into view, Maggie could see she was scared. She had put on her Snow White wig and was carrying her princess doll.

'Hi, Beth. Are you OK?' Maggie tried to sound upbeat and normal.

The girl nodded.

'Sam and me and this man, we've got to talk about things. Grown up things.'

Again Beth nodded. She walked across the room and gave Maggie a hug. Maggie could feel her tension. She would have liked to reassure her but the words wouldn't come. All she could do was whisper — five little words.

Beth gave a final squeeze and then ran back up the stairs as if the hounds of hell were after her. Maggie heard her slam a door shut. A patter of feet. Then silence.

'Where is it?' The man was leaning back in his chair, hands steepled together under his chin.

'What do I call you?' she said.

He considered the question, rubbing the tips of his fingers together. 'William.'

'William?' she laughed, mimicking his accent. 'I prefer Billy.' She could see he didn't like this. A man who hated to be mocked. A humourless bastard. They were all bastards.

'Well, Billy, maybe you should explain what it is you're looking for.'

'I think you know, Maggie.'

She shook her head. She wasn't sure what she was doing, what her strategy was, but playing hard to get was going to be part of it.

The pupils of Billy's eyes seemed to shrink even more. He slipped his hand inside his jacket and pulled out a small black gun. He set it down on the arm of his chair and placed his right hand next to it. 'Search her, Sam.'

Maggie stood up. Her legs were trembling. She waited while Sam frisked her. His hands lingered longer than they needed to on her legs, thighs, trunk and arse. She wanted to knee him in the crotch, but she didn't. She tried to focus only on his face as his fingers probed her pockets, where they found nothing except the car keys. He studied them before passing them over to his boss.

'What happened to Ellie?' she said to the man.

He glanced up at Sam. 'Didn't Sam tell you?'

'He told me a pack of lies. Why did you kill her?'

The smile was back on his podgy face. Insincere. Self-satisfied. Nasty. Was that the last thing she would ever see? Would she take that face to her grave? His vicious fat ball of a face, half overexposed in the bright sunlight, the other half sunk in shadow, peering across at her in this room that held so many good memories?

'Why would Sam lie to you?' he said, smooth as a rattlesnake. 'Ellie shot herself. But Sam didn't want Beth to live with that terrible knowledge. A traffic accident was a much kinder way of explaining it.'

'Do you think I'm an idiot? There's no reference to her death anywhere on the internet. People who blow their brains out usually get a mention. Someone comes across the body — someone walking a dog or training for a marathon or taking their kids for a picnic. And then the local papers report on it because it's much more interesting than a flower show that's been rained off.'

'We recovered the body. Tracked it through her mobile. So we took charge of her and saw she got a proper funeral.' He had all the answers. She distrusted people with all the answers. 'But we kept it out of the press because Sam wanted to protect Beth, like any father would.'

'So tell me why the hell Ellie would have killed herself and thereby abandon her daughter? Mothers don't do that.'

'You're an expert on motherhood are you, Maggie? Since when?' The jibe was a dagger slipped in between her ribs. Did he know? About her and the still-birth? That she would never, ever give birth again — even to another dead baby? She looked up at Sam. He knew that bit of her history. Had he told him? Or was she being paranoid? Sam was silhouetted against the window with the sun behind him, his expression hidden deep in the shadows. She had never been able to work him out. Not then. Certainly not now.

'More than you,' she said to Bowman, but so quietly that neither of them could possibly have heard. She had carried her baby for seven months. She knew what it was to be a mother. And she knew too with absolute certainty that Sam had betrayed her deepest secret to his boss.

* * *

The pain was less now. It still stabbed right up his leg every time Elgar put his foot down, but in between it was bearable. He was only a hundred metres or so from the cottage and although he was moving ridiculously slowly, the distance was getting less. The woman's car was still parked where it had been when they had arrived and there was no one in view which meant they had to be inside, though quite what state they would be in was anybody's guess. There would have been four bullets left in his gun after she had blown off his toe. Who knew what she might have done with them?

He tried to review his options. Bridget had held onto the car keys in her usual control-freak manner. So even if his right foot had been capable of controlling accelerator and break, the lack of a key ruled out driving off into the sunset. Staggering to the pub would involve another 300 metres of agony, so forget that. Which left one option: going into the cottage and seeing what the mess was there. If Maggie was in there and in charge, hopefully she wouldn't blow the big toe off his other foot.

He plodded on, trying not to limp more than he had to. Best not to attract the attention of curious villagers now they had reached the end game. As he got closer to the cottage, he saw movement through the front window. Then in an upstairs window he glimpsed a face which suddenly ducked out of sight. He kept his eyes on it as he pressed on and was rewarded by another, longer, glimpse. It had to be the girl. He was glad about that. The kid was OK. For now at least.

He didn't bother knocking. He took a deep breath, twisted the handle and pushed his way in.

Three sets of eyes swivelled towards him. Bowman, Sam and the woman.

It was Bowman who spoke. 'Elgar, how nice to see you. I would introduce you to Maggie, but I think you've already met.' Not a word about the blood all over his sock.

Elgar moved gingerly towards the dining table and grabbed the back of a chair. Now that he was inside, there was no need to pretend. The pain was taking on a new and virulent life of its own, jabbing at his foot like an angry scorpion. He wanted to tell them this but all he did was give the chair a violent twist and then slump onto it with a gasp of relief.

'I think I need some medical care,' he said.

'What happened?' Bowman asked the obvious question, but he didn't seem to be interested in the answer. His attention was clearly elsewhere — on Maggie, to judge from the way he was glaring at her — and maybe on how to clear up the bloody mess over which he was presiding.

'She blew my big toe off.' Elgar tried to lift his foot, but a stab of pain made him stop. He looked around the room. The woman, Maggie, was sitting absolutely still, her eyes fixed on Bowman. She was not, he now knew, a woman to be underestimated. Sam stood with his back to the window, silent and in shadow, so it was hard to read his face. Elgar didn't trust him. He wasn't sure why, but what little he had seen of the man disturbed him. If he was the kid's father, how come he was so cool about the situation?

'Maybe you should retire,' Bowman said. 'If you can't carry out the simplest of orders, then you're clearly past your sell-by date. And where the hell is Bridget? And the old man?'

'Didn't she tell you?' Elgar gestured towards Maggie.

'She claimed they were both dead.'

'That's right. They are.'

* * *

Beth was sitting on Maggie's bed. It was a double bed. She liked double beds. She had loved sneaking into her mum's in the night, even though her mum had told her she was getting too big for it.

'You let Sam sleep in it,' she said one time, 'and he is much bigger than me.'

'That's different,' she had said. But she had never explained how it was different. Did that mean she loved Sam more than she loved her own daughter? Beth hadn't

165

dared to ask her that question, but it sat there in her head nevertheless.

She bounced quietly on the bed. It was very soft. She wondered if Maggie would allow her to sleep in it with her.

There was a big wardrobe with mirrors on both doors. She had been going to hide in it, but when she had run back to the house, she had found Sam and the man inside, so there hadn't been any need. Sam had been really odd. He seemed cross that she was there. He had snapped at her and told her to stay upstairs, but then Maggie had arrived and he had called her down to say "hello" to her and then he had sent her upstairs again.

Maggie had given her a hug and told her not to worry. Beth had wanted the hug to last for ever. She felt safe with Maggie. Maggie wasn't going to be pushed around by anyone. Maggie wasn't going to go out one evening and never come home.

The hug hadn't lasted for ever, but just before Maggie let her go she had whispered some words in her ear. 'What would you do, Beth?' Which was exactly what they had been talking about earlier, when they had their picnic in the quarry.

Maggie had told her about the game they'd played when she was small. 'What would you do?' her father had asked her when they were staying in a windmill. Maggie had told her how she and her brother had decided that the best way to escape if the windmill caught fire was to climb out of the window onto one of the sails and then wait until they got close to the ground before jumping off.

Obviously this wasn't a windmill. It was a little cottage. But she *was* trapped upstairs. She couldn't go down the stairs because Maggie and Sam and the two other men were right at the bottom. She had looked out of the window at the front and she had seen the man who had chased Maggie limping towards the house. He had looked very cross and she was pretty sure he had seen her. Then there was also the fat man with thick-rimmed glasses who had been sitting in the armchair when she had arrived back at the house. He had spoken with a horrid squeaky voice. 'Go and wait in your bedroom, little girl. And don't come down until I say so.'

There was no way out of the front window. She had read a book once in which a girl had climbed into a big old house up the ivy to see if the old lady who lived there had kidnapped her dog, but there was no ivy here.

She picked up her rucksack and slipped it onto her back. She looked around the room. What should she do? Maggie had hung her dressing gown on the back of the door. She went over and pulled its cord out of its loops. Then she opened the door and listened. She could hear someone talking — one of the men. She tiptoed along the little corridor past the bathroom and into her little bedroom. Quiet as a mouse she shut the door behind her. She was good at being quiet as a mouse. Mum used to tell her so. She went over to the window, very carefully pulled the handle down and pushed the window open. She peered out. There was no ivy here either. There was a nice little garden: a lawn which hadn't been cut recently, three circular beds containing a cheerful mixture of pink, white and blue flowers, and there were various bushes and four trees. It was all enclosed by a wooden fence. It was too tall to climb. She scanned it carefully. Wasn't there a gate? How would she get out? Then she saw it, half-hidden by the dappled shadows under the two trees at the far end of the garden.

What would you do?

There was no ivy to climb down and no windmill sail to grab hold of, but there was a roof below her. It was the roof of the kitchen and its top wasn't very far below her window. But what if she fell? But she had already thought of this. There were two pillows on her bed and a duvet. She had laid out her dressing gown for the evening, but she wasn't sure she would need it now. She pulled the cord out of it and tied it to the one from Maggie's. All she had to do was put one pillow on her front and one on her back and then tie them on tight with the cords. Then if she fell, she would be protected. But doing that was easier said than done and Beth soon realised she couldn't do it on her own.

What now? Maggie had told her always have a plan B, in case plan A doesn't work. Beth grabbed the duvet off the bed and lowered it from the window. If she could get it onto the roof and then lower herself onto it, she could wrap it around herself in case she slipped and maybe she wouldn't get too hurt. She said a little prayer and let the duvet go. It dropped onto the apex of the roof, but instead of settling there like a blanket of snow it slithered down the roof and onto the ground below.

For a moment, Beth thought she was going to cry, but then she heard one of the men shouting downstairs. She had to escape. She grabbed both pillows. Suppose she put both arms in them? She tried it, slipping her hands deep into the pillow cases, but immediately realised that she wouldn't be able to hold onto anything. She threw them down.

What now? All she had was her rucksack and the dressing gown cords. And the bed! What would you do? It was as if Maggie was there with her. Quickly she knotted one end of the cord around the brass end of the bed and tugged at it. It seemed firm. She clambered up onto the window ledge and sat down on it, her legs dangling outside. She looked down at the roof. It wasn't far. She counted to three, eased herself round, tightened the cord and began to lower herself. She had done rope climbing at school. She could do this. She knew she could. Unless she had miscalculated. The cord wasn't that long. She felt a moment of panic, a moment when she almost cried out and then her feet felt the safety of the roof below her. Except, of course, she wasn't safe yet.

She held onto the cord, not letting go until she was perched astride the apex of the roof. She turned round and began to edge forwards. She tried not to think of the men in the house. If they saw her, they would shout, but they weren't shouting so she was OK. She got to the end of the roof and peered down. She had hoped there would be a big soft bush to fall into at the end of the kitchen, but there wasn't. Just a patio with a rusty barbecue. She would have to slide down the roof and hope for the best. On one side was the lawn, and she was pretty sure they would be able to see her if she fell there, and on the other side there was a wheelie bin.

She paused, counted to one, and slid towards the wheelie bin.

She landed right on top of it. It was a bit like gymnastics except that the bin was no vaulting horse. She felt it wobble beneath her, but she twisted with her hips and pushed with her hands and, just as Miss Grant had taught her, she landed four-square on the ground, flexing her legs as she did so. The wheelie bin stayed upright. She paused and held her breath. There was no noise from the house, no shouting. Crouching low, she ran along the side of the garden and up to the back gate. There was a bolt on it. It was coated with rust. She tried to slide it open, but it wouldn't budge. She pulled with all her might, but it remained jammed tight. She turned round, scouring the garden. No one was coming out of the house. And there was another gate! She ran back down the garden, past the wheelie bin and tried the bolt on that gate. This time it slid easily. She opened the gate carefully, edged forward and looked round the corner of the house. No one. Crouching even lower she ran under the front windows and then down the lane towards the village. She knew only one person in the village, Mrs Sidebottom. She remembered the funny name and that she had been nice. She ran a shop out of the back of the pub. She wasn't quite sure what that meant but she would go there and get her to help. Mrs Sidebottom would ring the police and then everything would be alright.

She ran like the wind. She ran like a jaguar, the fastest animal in the world. She ran like a lamplighter. That was what her mum had said after sports day, 'You ran like a lamplighter, love. I'm proud of you.' Beth reached the pub, pushed the door open and stumbled in. 'Mrs Sidebottom!' she cried and hurled herself at the woman. 'There are bad men trying to kill us! Call the police.'

She felt Mrs Sidebottom's arms around her, warm and comforting and safe. She wished they were Ellie's or Maggie's, but Mrs Sidebottom was the next best thing.

Then she heard a man's voice. 'You must be Beth.'

She turned round. There were two men and she didn't know who either of them was.

'Don't worry,' the other man said. He was a big man with a very short haircut and a deep voice. His face was red and shiny with sweat. 'We're policemen. We'll look after you.'

Beth screamed.

* * *

Elgar was perched on his chair, trying not to fall off it. The excruciating flashes of pain in his foot had given way a deep throbbing which reverberated halfway up his leg. He was feeling faint, so faint that if he tried to stand up he was pretty sure he would fall. He shut his eyes, trying to combat the feelings of dizziness and nausea which were threatening to engulf him. He wondered if the others had noticed. Or if they had, whether they cared.

He tried to tune back into the conversation. Maggie was talking, very definite and much louder than necessary. 'I haven't got whatever it is you think I've got.'

'Why did you go to the quarry, Maggie?' That was Bowman. Elgar recognised that calm, reasonable tone. It was a danger sign. When he was calm, quiet and reasonable, that was the time to beware.

'It's a lovely day. Beth and I went there for a picnic.'

'Like you and Ellie once did?'

Was that a guess? Or did he know that for a fact? Elgar opened his eyes, relieved that the nausea had subsided somewhat. He flexed his fingers, focusing on them in an attempt to distract himself from his leg.

'Like my father and I did when I was a child.' Maggie wasn't crumbling or backing down. She had dropped her voice, mimicking Bowman, and she stared back at him, unblinking. Elgar wondered if she was scared. She ought to be. But if she was, she was hiding it very effectively.

'Ah! Very cute. A trip down memory lane, was it? For old time's sake?'

She nodded.

'Don't make me laugh.' Bowman hissed the words through barely parted lips. He sat there in the armchair, returning her gaze. Elgar couldn't help but see him as a cobra, waiting to strike. Mesmerising and deadly.

'I don't suppose you ever laugh,' she replied. Elgar tried not to smile. This woman could give as good as she got. She was not to be underestimated, he told himself again. He had done precisely that, and now he was missing a big toe. But he doubted that Bowman would make the same mistake.

Silence. If Bowman was a cobra, maybe she was a mongoose, waiting her turn to strike. He remembered watching a duel between a cobra and a mongoose on some wildlife programme, but he couldn't remember which of animal had won.

Bowman shifted in his chair, sitting more upright and casting the briefest of glances up at Sam.

'Bring Beth down here,' he ordered.

Elgar saw Maggie start as she too glanced at Sam. He noted the alarm in her face and the tightening of her hands. Bowman had found her weak spot.

No one moved or said a thing. Impasse. Was this the still before the storm, the moment before all hell broke loose? Even Sam, standing rigid in the shadows, seemed to be considering whether to obey Bowman.

'Now!' Bowman snapped.

Sam grunted. He started to move, across the room and up the stairs.

'Beth!' he called as he got to the top. Elgar heard him open one door, then another. Sam called the girl's name again. He swore.

Elgar glanced sideways and saw Bowman pick up his gun. He pointed it towards Maggie. 'Don't even think of moving, darling.'

Then there was a heavy clumping of feet as Sam came down the stairs much quicker than he had gone up.

'She's scarpered.' His face was red with fury. 'The girl's escaped out the back window. God only knows where she is.'

'We'll have to do this without her.' Bowman rose to his feet and edged round to the side of the sofa, his eyes and gun fixed on Maggie. 'Tell me what I need to know and you are free to go, you and the girl — if you can find her. Otherwise I'll kill you first and then I'll find her and kill her.'

Maggie stood up. 'You'd kill a little girl, would you? To cover your back?' Elgar watched with fascination. She was a tough cookie, there was no doubt of that. 'What sort of man are you?'

'Sit down, Maggie.' Bowman spoke one syllable at a time. He was pointing the gun straight at her. 'Nobody need get hurt. As long as you cooperate.'

For three or four seconds, there was stalemate. Then Maggie lowered herself back into the chair.

'Let me do it.' Elgar held out his hand. Bowman looked at him. Elgar continued, 'She blew my toe off, so I'll blow her toe off, and then I'll put one through her kneecap if she doesn't cooperate and then . . .' He paused as a grin spread across his face. 'Well, I'll find some other part of her to blow off until she does spill the beans.'

Bowman frowned. He looked down at the gun in his hand and across the room at Maggie.

Elgar snarled. 'For God's sake, give me the gun. Do we have the time to piss about?'

Bowman opened his mouth as if to say something, then changed his mind. He gave Elgar the gun.

Elgar hefted it in his hand. It was too light and small for him, but at this range it was more than adequate. He lifted the gun and fired. He was aiming to miss, but whether it was the pain that had started to shoot up his leg again or the unfamiliar gun, the bullet scraped the side of Maggie's left shoulder. She screamed and slapped her right hand over it. 'I haven't got the damned memory stick! I threw it in the lake in the quarry. You'll never find it.'

'Liar!' It was Bowman, his face taut with rage. 'Why would you have thrown it in the lake?'

'I panicked.'

Bowman pursed his lips. 'Skip the big toe,' he said quietly. 'Just do the kneecap. On the count of three. One. Two—'

Bowman never got to three. The word froze somewhere at the back of his throat. Elgar swivelled round. He had had enough. Of obeying orders. Of inflicting pain and death. Of being trampled on. He raised the gun and pointed it at Bowman's head. He paused just long enough to see the fear blossom on Bowman's face. Another stab of pain shot up his leg, but his hand was steady. Bowman opened his mouth, but Elgar didn't hear what he said. He clenched his teeth. There would be no way back after this. He squeezed the trigger and a single bullet punched a hole clean through Bowman's forehead.

* * *

They didn't run. Ashcroft had wanted to, that was his nature, but Reid had grabbed his arm and forced him to stop. Reid insisted on walking out of the village towards the holiday cottage. He moved briskly, anxious not to waste time, weighing up the options and possibilities. That was *his* nature.

Neither of them had a gun, they were miles away from back-up and they had no idea what on earth they were going to encounter. The girl had gabbled about two people dead in the quarry and how a bad man was holding Maggie hostage in the cottage and the bad man had a gun. As far as Reid was concerned, there were two options. Wait or go in. But he hadn't flogged all over the country just to hang around waiting. So they had to go in. Again there appeared to be various options: they could barge in through the front door like a pair of bull elephants. Or they could creep round the side and see if there was a back door that had been left conveniently unlocked. Or they could knock on the front door like a pair of Jehovah's Witnesses, and see who answered it. Reid blew his cheeks out and pressed on a little faster. When you thought about it, most of the available options ruled themselves out.

'I'll go first,' Reid said as the cottage came into view.

Ashcroft grunted, though Reid didn't know what this meant. Not that it bothered him. For all his faults, Ashcroft was a good person to have at your back when you were in a tricky situation. He might be a slimy creep in the office, but Ashcroft was the sort of man who came alive when faced by a killer with a gun.

They slowed as they drew near. Reid ran his eyes over the building — small, four-square, red brick and rather out of place here. He had expected a pretty country cottage with a flurry of wild flowers decorating the front garden, stone walls, even a thatched roof. Not that he had time to take it all in. What he was looking for were signs of life. The side gate was open, swinging slightly in the breeze. He peered hard at the windows. He thought he could see shadows moving inside.

He crossed the last few metres and knocked on the door. He heard raised voices, a conversation of sorts, followed by the sound of a bolt being slid aside. The door opened and a tall man with a disarming smile looked down at him. 'Can I help?'

Reid recognised Sam Foulkes immediately. He had seen so many pictures of him he could have drawn him with his eyes shut. He had even encountered him a couple of times, or rather passed him in the corridor without knowing who the heck he was. It was impossible to walk past a man that tall and not notice him. He had heard the rumours too, and he had read enough about him to know that he wasn't to be trusted.

Reid smiled and held up his ID card, doing his best to portray himself as the friendly trustworthy detective. 'Hello, there. Do you mind if we come in?'

This was the moment when he had half expected Foulkes to produce a gun or other weapon, but Foulkes merely nodded and turned. The two of them followed him inside. Reid knew it could be a trap. Most probably it was a trap. The fact that Foulkes wasn't waving a gun under his nose meant absolutely nothing. There were other people inside. Probably one of them had a gun poised in his or her hand. The likelihood of the house being a gun-free zone was zero.

There was a woman sitting in an armchair. Reid recognised her too. It was Maggie Rogers. She was pale and her eyes were darting around the room as if they were trying to track down a hyperactive mosquito. She didn't appear to have a gun either.

In fact, the only gun was lying on the floor. A man's hand was wrapped round it, but there was no danger of him firing it because he was extremely dead. Reid wondered who it was. Possibly he knew him, but there was so little of his face left that it was impossible to tell. Suicide, the scenario said. But maybe it said it a little too obviously.

'Hell! It's Bowman,' Ashcroft said. He was crouching down behind the sofa over another body. At least Reid assumed it was a body. From where he stood all he could see was a pair of feet with highly polished black laced shoes sticking out from behind the sofa. He moved around to get a better look.

'He's dead,' Ashcroft said, unnecessarily. The small hole in the middle of his forehead and the huge wound at the back of his head were eloquent enough.

Both detectives turned and faced the only two other people still alive in the room. Maggie was still sitting absolutely motionless in the chair. Reid guessed that she was in shock. Foulkes had moved behind her and was resting a hand on her shoulder, as if to reassure her.

'I think you had better tell us what happened,' Reid said.

CHAPTER EIGHT

Reid had been waiting for half an hour. He wished he had accepted the offer of a cup of coffee from the immaculately dressed young man who had escorted him up from the reception area and was now sitting at a desk on the other side of the room, doing things on his computer. The huge computer screen mostly hid him from view, but even so, Reid couldn't shake off the feeling that the young man was keeping a very careful watch on him.

Reid was tempted to play solitaire on his phone. Whenever he was stressed or bored, he had a tendency to retreat into solitaire. It was a great way to shut out the rest of the world.

He was feeling stressed *and* bored now. Stressed because he had been summoned to meet Mark Ruskin, a man so far up the pyramid of power that he probably needed an oxygen mask. Reid had never met him before. Bowman had mentioned him once, in tones which marked him out as someone to be avoided at all costs. Reid was bored because the only reading material on the coffee table in front of him was a copy of the *Financial Times*. If there was ever an occasion to retreat inside a game of solitaire, this was it. Except that playing solitaire in this place would have felt frivolous and dangerous, like pushing a stick inside a wasps' nest and stirring it around to see what happened. He had done that once as a boy and had ended up with an ear the size of an elephant's.

So Reid sat still and let his mind drift back to the day of Bowman's death. The woman, Maggie, had barely spoken a word. At the time Reid had put it down to shock and he hadn't changed his mind since. The only thing she had said was to ask if the girl — Beth — was alright. Reid had reassured her. 'Thank God for that,' she had said and relapsed into a silence which she had not broken for three days.

Sam Foulkes had been anything but silent. He had been rather hyper. He had described in rapid detail how Maggie had arrived at the house in a state of distress. How he had persuaded Beth to go upstairs and play in her bedroom so that they could have a proper discussion with Maggie. How Maggie had told them about this guy trying to kill her in the quarry. She had escaped from him, even managed to club him on the head with a rock. But then, suddenly, he had burst in waving a gun and threatening to kill them all. Sam said he had no idea who the guy was.

'At first I thought he was a bit of a fruitcake. Bowman must have thought so too. He started to talk him down, persuade him to drop the gun. He was doing a good job. I thought the guy was going to put it down on the table, but then it was like someone had flipped a switch. The guy's face froze. He raised his arm, pointed the gun at Bowman and pulled the trigger. Puff! Straight through the forehead. I should have acted then, thrown myself at him. But he was ice-cool. He turned the gun on me, told me to sit down and then he raised the gun up to his own head, just under the chin and pulled the trigger again. Jesus, I nearly wet myself!'

'Inspector Reid!' The immaculately tailored young man was standing in front of him, breaking into his reverie. 'Mr Ruskin will see you now.' Reid stood up. Ben led the way over to a door in the middle of the oak-panelled wall and opened it. With a nod, he directed Reid through the opening into Ruskin's inner sanctum. Reid advanced forward. He heard the door click shut behind him and wondered for the twenty-ninth time that morning what the hell this meeting was all about.

'Come in and sit down!' The voice emanated from the corner of the room. Reid assumed it was Ruskin, but the man's back was turned towards him. The man turned round. He had a cup of coffee in his hand and he held it out to Reid. 'Here,' he said. 'Keep me company.'

Soon they were sitting opposite each other, on either side of a ridiculously large desk of the sort Reid had only ever seen on TV or in National Trust houses.

'Detective Inspector Reid.' Ruskin sipped at his coffee. 'You're probably wondering why I wanted to see you. Well, first of all I want to thank you. You're a very professional man. I've read your personnel files. Lots of very positive comments over the years. And of course you did a fine job the other day.' He paused and smiled at Reid, who felt uncomfortable. He had no doubt that this was the buttering-up part of the interview. The lull before the storm. 'It was all very unfortunate,' Ruskin continued. 'Bowman was a very fine officer, one of my best, totally loyal and reliable. But to be shot by a lunatic with a gun who then turned the gun on himself.' Ruskin took another sip of coffee. 'Now that really is a desperate end.'

Reid sipped at his own coffee. Normally he liked coffee, but this tasted like mud.

'You submitted a report, of course. Quite right. Senior officer on the scene.'

Reid knew what was coming. In general terms if not in detail. He would have to be a grade A idiot to not realise what it was: a very large 'but.' With a capital 'B.'

'I have to say I am not entirely comfortable with your conclusions.' Ruskin faced him, elbows on the desk, hands clenched together, chin resting on top of them, eyes staring.

Reid knew he had to say something. Ruskin's silence was as insistent as the Napoleon clock on his desk, ticking remorselessly onwards.

'My conclusions were based on my assessment of the evidence.' Reid winced as he heard the words come out. Was that the best he could do?

'Your conclusions were highly speculative.' Ruskin spoke sharply. 'Subjective too, Inspector. Not what I would have expected of an officer of your experience.' His Adam's apple bobbed in his throat. 'I would go so far as to say that it is a very damaging report. Damaging for the reputation of a very able officer who is under my ultimate control.' He paused. His eyes tightened. 'And potentially very damaging to you, as the officer who submitted it.'

Reid tried not to flinch, but he was out of his depth, treading water and not having a clue how far his feet were from the bottom.

'Did you know the man who shot Bowman?' Ruskin said.

'No, I don't think so.' Reid cleared his throat. 'What I mean to say is, his face was one hell of a mess. He would have been hard to identify even if he had been a colleague or a friend. He had no ID on him.'

Ruskin was still watching him, eyes half closed.

Reid blundered on. Now that he had started, he couldn't stop. 'Which was what made me suspicious. Everyone has ID with them these days. A bank card at least. Most people have endless cards — coffee shop cards, store cards, driving licence . . . But not him. Which meant someone had taken it off him. And there were only two people who could have done that.'

'I see.'

'And then there was another thing. The entry point of the bullet which killed him was under the left-hand side of the jaw. He was right-handed. You could tell because his watch was on his left hand. It would have been very difficult for him to position the gun where it must have been positioned.'

'I've read your report very thoroughly, Inspector.' Ruskin stood up and brushed imaginary dust off his jacket. Then he looked across at Reid. 'I still hold to the view that it is flawed. I have therefore ordered that it be removed from the system. As from today, you are on gardening leave. You are not to return to your office. I have arranged for a letter to be delivered to your home address within the next twenty-four hours. It will contain full details of the terms of your early retirement. You are not to discuss this with anyone. You are also not to attempt to make any contact with your former colleague, Detective Inspector Ashcroft. Is that clear?'

Reid nodded. Detective Inspector Ashcroft! The message could hardly be clearer.

'In that case, goodbye and enjoy your retirement.'

* * *

Reid had never been in shock before. Was this what it was like? He had made it to the embankment on the edge of the Thames without any consciousness of how he got there. One moment he was being escorted back out of the building by the young clothes horse and the next he was here, leaning against the wall and staring across the water. He looked around and his eyes settled on a Chinese bride and her groom. They were perched on the embankment wall. A man with a camera on a tripod was busy framing them against the background of the Houses of Parliament while another man and a woman fussed over the bride's dress and hair. The groom was looking intently at his mobile phone.

The woman Maggie had been in shock — or so he had assumed — sitting frozen on her chair, almost catatonic. Perhaps she too had been unable to understand how on earth she had got there. One minute she had been out there on the moors with the girl and the next there in the cottage in the middle of a bloodbath.

Samuel Foulkes had got away with it. Reid knew that now. He had shot the guy who had shot Bowman. Only that explained all the discrepancies. He should have challenged him at the time, searched him, but he hadn't been sure what he had blundered into until much later, when he had lain sleepless in bed and put everything together. 'A very able officer under my ultimate control.' That had been what Ruskin had said. It had been a warning. But it had also been an admission. 'Ultimate control.' Why ultimate? Who was he referring to? He had assumed at the time that he was referring to Bowman, but the only way the words made sense were if they referred to Sam Foulkes. Sam Foulkes was an undercover officer whom Ruskin wanted to protect. Back off, Reid, had been the message. Or else. And stupid fool that he was, he had been reluctant to back off.

Reid looked around again. He couldn't help feeling that someone was watching him. The Chinese wedding group was still there. There were individuals and couples walking towards him along the embankment. He looked the other way. A group of elderly people were advancing towards him from the opposite direction. He wondered what had brought them here today. He began to walk towards them. He needed a good long walk while he tried to come to terms with his new status. Gardening leave, and soon after that a prolonged retirement stretching far into the distance until cancer or a heart attack or pneumonia put an end to the regular monthly payments.

He moved to the right, allowing the crowd of pensioners to pass by him. There were a few smiles and acknowledgements, as if to say welcome to the club.

'Excuse me.' He recoiled as a woman brushed past him. She was going in the same direction, but much more briskly. He admired her figure. She wore a green coat with a brown belt pulled tight, as if to emphasise her slim waist.

Tan boots. Light brown hair which flowed behind her. He felt a yearning for a life lived and lost, for the vigour of youth which he would never experience again. He willed her to stop and turn around. He wanted to see her face, to see her smile or scowl or merely look bemused.

There was a noise behind him. Reid turned to see a cyclist, togged up with all the latest gear — shorts, hi vis shirt, helmet, mask over his face against the London pollution — only metres away. He raised his right hand. There was something in it which flashed in the sunlight. A knife?

Reid ducked and pulled his arms across over his head. He was ready for the sudden pain, but he wasn't going to go quietly. He heard the squeal of brakes and a thump as the cycle hit the stonework.

'What the hell are you playing at?'

Reid looked up. The man staring down at him his was furious. His left hand gripped his bike, the right a mobile phone.

'You bloody idiot!'

The man straightened his cycle and pedalled off.

Reid leant against the parapet, waiting for the feelings of panic and paranoia to subside.

In the distance, the Chinese bride and groom were still there, still trying to get the perfect photographs to commemorate their perfect wedding. Silently Reid wished them well and began to trudge in the opposite direction. Early retirement. Peace. No more stupid work schedules. No more internal politics. Leave that to Ashcroft. Perhaps Mark Ruskin had done him a favour after all.

* * *

In the end Maggie came clean with Sam and handed over the USB stick to him.

He stared at it for several seconds before stuffing it into his pocket.

'That proves nothing,' he said. 'You've probably made a copy of it.'

'I haven't.'

'That's a solemn promise, is it? Cross your heart and hope to die?'

'I'm not interested in pursuing justice or righting wrongs.'

'What are you interested in then, Maggs?'

'I'm only interested in Beth.'

He nodded, but said nothing.

'The deal is that I look after Beth and you stay out of our lives.'

Again he nodded.

'That means starting now! While Beth is asleep. You take your bag and you don't come back. Ever.'

There was a long pause. Sam raised himself to his feet and stretched his arms. 'OK. But I need to say goodbye to her.'

'Don't wake her up.'

'I won't.'

'Good.'

Maggie waited silently while he said his goodbyes to Beth and then herself. She allowed him to hug her, but that was all. She waited for him to disengage and when he had gone she locked and bolted the door firmly behind him. She stood at the window and watched his tall shape recede into the darkness. Off back to his other life.

Maggie had gone through every file on the USB. She had seen all the photos from Sam's other life. A woman and two teenage boys. Him and a scruffy terrier. Sam at a police training college. She had seen other images too. Of unidentifiable dead men and in one case a dead woman. Of Sam talking to the man she now knew to have been Bowman. And finally there had been a photo of the gravestone of a little boy who had died thirty-six years previously on his fifth birthday. The gravestone of Samuel Foulkes. The little boy whose identity Sam had stolen.

That was the evidence that Ellie had gathered and had threatened to use against them. And that was why she had ended up dead.

Maggie's phone rang. She started. Who on earth would be ringing her? Who knew her number now? Only one person. She answered the call. It was always best to face things head on.

'It's me. Sam.'

She swore.

'Look, I just need to tell you. I want you to know that I never knew they intended to kill Ellie. I would never have let them. You've got to believe me.'

'Goodbye, Sam.'

'Do you believe me?' She could hear the desperation in his voice.

'I do,' she said.

'Thank God,' he said.

Maggie terminated the call.

She had to believe him. Or she would never have peace.

* * *

Maggie believed in fresh starts. She had made them before and if necessary she would do so again. This was her first ever trip to Cornwall, and already she knew she would be happy. They would both be happy. Beth was building a sandcastle several metres away. She had been doing it for over an hour and it was a wonderful thing to behold: a tall central structure with four small turrets on top, a wall all around it, a moat around the wall and shells studding everything. Beth was sitting cross-legged inside the walls. She had stopped building now. She was waiting for the tide to come in. In half an hour or so, the castle would cease to exist. But that didn't matter. They could come back tomorrow and Beth could build another one.

Sam had been relieved to pass all responsibility over to her. He had insisted that Beth was not his daughter.

'Ellie never said she was mine, not once. She would have said, now wouldn't she?' Maybe Ellie just didn't know. Certainly Sam didn't want to know. 'What about DNA testing?' Maggie had suggested, and he had thrown up his hands in horror.

'What the hell would be the point? Look, the fact is I would never make a good father. Ellie is gone, so Beth needs a new mother, and I reckon you are as good as anyone.'

Maggie wasn't sure that *good* was the right word. She knew she would be a good mother. No one would ever harm Beth while she was around to protect her. She would teach her to look after herself and to learn the ways of the world. But she wasn't sure that *good* was a word that she could otherwise apply to herself. Not when she had killed a man as cold-bloodedly as she had.

The man's name was Elgar. Sam had told her that later. Elgar had saved her and Beth from Bowman. He had shot him clean through the head, spattering his brains all over the wall behind him. But then Elgar had aimed the gun at Sam and forced him onto his knees. 'Don't trust him, Maggie,' Sam had insisted. 'I know him. I know what he's done.'

Elgar had perched on the arm of the sofa. He must have lost a lot of blood.

'I'll cover him,' she had said. 'Give me the gun and I'll make sure Sam doesn't move. You ring for help.' Elgar had taken a bit of persuading, but in the end he had agreed. He had been relieved to let her take over. He had started to shiver. She told him not to worry. 'I've got some medical training. Let me take a look at your foot.' So he had sunk down into the sofa and just for a second or two he had closed his eyes. That had been long enough. She had placed the gun against his jaw and pulled the trigger.

'Mother!' A child was calling. Maggie looked around. She hadn't noticed any other kids with mothers. It was term time and they would all be at school. Just as Beth ought to be. Would be just as soon as they settled in properly, once they had bonded. Maggie wondered whether she should home-school Beth for a while. Lots of people did it these days.

'Mother!' The child called again. Maggie looked around again and realised with a start that it was Beth who was calling. 'Mother!'

She felt a lurch of delight and pushed herself up onto her feet. 'Coming, darling!'

'Quick, Mother, before the tide comes in.'

THE END

Thank you for reading this book. If you enjoyed it please leave feedback on Amazon, and if there is anything we missed or you have a question about then please get in touch. The author and publishing team appreciate your feedback and time reading this book.

Our email is office@joffebooks.com

www.joffebooks.com

ALSO BY PETER TICKLER

DEAD IN THE WATER

Made in the USA
San Bernardino, CA
04 June 2017